# DISHWASHER SAFE

# BY RICK SHEFFIELD

## SEVERE CLEAR
## PUBLISHING

MW01532381

Dishwasher Safe
By Rick Sheffield
Copyright 2024 by Rick Sheffield
ISBN: 979-8-218-32528-2

All rights reserved
Printed in the United States of America

No part of this book may be used or reproduced in any manner whatsoever without the written permission of the author except in the case of brief quotations embodied in critical articles and reviews.

This novel is purely fictitious. Any similarity to real persons, living or dead, is coincidental. The peculiar events described herein are inspired by decades of interacting with many outrageous characters, but all names and products are as real as the notion of free shipping.

Cover Design by Eric Labacz, labaczdesign.com

Published by Severe Clear Publishing

*In memory of my big brother Skip,*
*a writer and musician*
*who gleefully resisted the dreadful pull of*
*normalcy.*

# CHAPTER 1

"Quiet on the set. And action!"

The perky blond on-camera talent for the infomercial sprang to work. The product was an amazing new mop with "cyclonic action." She gamely tried to maneuver the whirling contraption over a piece of carpet that had been purposefully soiled with dirt and soot to make it look like the floor of a pigsty. The mop shot out of her hand and knocked over a light stand with a crash. Filthy, sudsy water flew everywhere. The spinning "cyclonic" brushes broke free of the machine and sailed like Frisbees across the room as everyone on the set ducked to avoid being beheaded.

"Cut," shouted the director. "Let's take a breather. That's ten minutes, people." The young crew of college interns eagerly pulled out their cellphones to check messages and text friends while a production assistant cleaned up the mess. Some grazed at a table of day-old doughnuts and tepid coffee. The production facility was actually part of a vocational school which made it the cheapest studio in town to rent.

"Sorry, Dickie," said the blonde, brushing suds off her yellow pantsuit. "It won't washie-washie."

"It's not your fault, Summer. That thing's got some bugs to work out." Dick Lance, the director of this production, let out a sigh. He was behind schedule, the product was a miserable failure, and he needed to have a finished spot in twenty-four hours. It was time to start improvising.

Dick Lance was no stranger to "TV magic." After dropping out of college fifteen years before, he had answered a want ad for a production assistant at a small-market Ohio TV station. Even in the digital era, there is still a sprinkling of small market TV stations that help fuel the local economy with ads for car dealers, hardware stores, and plumbing services. Dick worked as a cameraman, audio man, set builder, floor sweeper—whatever was needed to keep their low-budget productions going.

After the Saturday morning cartoons, a yoga instructor bought a half-hour time slot to give yoga lessons and plug her studio. On Sunday afternoons a realtor showed slides of homes for sale in the area. The same obviously fake plastic plants moved from one set to another. These types of homespun productions kept the place afloat, if only barely.

One Sunday morning the weekend weatherman was a no-show.

Again.

He was so badly hungover he couldn't stand without puking and wisely called in sick. The Switcher who called the shots for the Sunday Morning News asked Dick if he would like to give the weather a try. Nothing to it. Just read the teleprompter and smile.

A megawatt lightbulb had gone off in Dick's head. He thought it over for all of twenty seconds. He'd always been an extrovert with an ego the size of Cleveland, and this was just what he had been hoping for. He was constantly imitating announcers he had heard and would bring ad copy home from the TV station to practice his delivery. In high school he had been voted Class Clown for his impersonations of late-night comedians, so he definitely wasn't shy. It didn't hurt that he had All-American Boy good looks, too.

Dick borrowed a tie, straightened his hair, and read through the weather report a few times before stepping in front of the camera. A red light lit, and the camera operator signaled that he was "on."

Dick was a natural. He gushed about the current good weather, then became deadly serious about the possibility of showers coming up by midweek, then poured on a big smile for improvements by the next weekend.

Suddenly Dick was the new weekend weatherman, and he had a new name. The station management decided his real name, Gorshenblatt, didn't have enough panache, so Dick Lance was born. As he honed his craft over the next few years and his ratings rose, he earned the regular evening news slot with a hefty raise in pay. He even came up with "Dick's Picks" at the end of the weather segment to spotlight the nation's best weather towns. Dick Lance became his legal name, and Gorshenblatt was never heard of again.

\*\*\*

"How do I work that thingy-thingy?" whined Summer Springfield, staring at the new replacement mop everyone hoped would make it through the shoot. Her pantsuit had dried out, her makeup had been reapplied, and she was ready to try again. Dick Lance patiently explained that the machine was a piece of shit that didn't work as advertised, so they were going to fake it.

"You just go through the motions and smile big. We'll do cutaways to make it look like the thing worked. We'll fix it in editing. You're a knockout baby; show me those pearly whites. Let's do this!"

The crew took their places, and the camera rolled. This time the emphasis was on Summer's smiling face, which would later be quickly cut to a sparkling clean carpet. Amazing!

After numerous takes, the production was over. The crew gave a sigh of relief and began to tear down the set. Summer gathered her makeup bag and made her way over to Dick, who was jotting down notes on the master script, trying to figure out how to make this hodgepodge of shots somehow believable. She waited a moment for him to acknowledge her but finally cleared her throat.

"Umm...Dick...are we okay?"

"Sure, sure, everything went fine. I'm going to lengthen the animation to cover those blown shots. Nobody's going to notice anything, believe me."

"I mean, are we okay for tonight?" She edged a little closer and caressed his arm, her lips parted in a manner she hoped would be wildly seductive. She had always worried that her lips were too thin and came close to getting Botox injections, but Dick talked her out of it saying he didn't want her to look like a balloon animal. He gave a sigh of exasperation.

"Oh, jeez, no. Not tonight. I'm gonna be up all night with the editor on this pile of crap. You know how it is; I've gotta put earrings on a pig."

"Are you calling me a pig?" she asked in mock alarm. "You'd better apol."

"No, no, of course not. You're being silly." Dick took

her hand and looked around to see who might be watching. "I've got a hard deadline with this thing, I've got writing to do, a shitload of voiceovers, there's just no time."

Summer's lips went into full pout mode. "It's okay. It's not a must can do."

Dick's voice dropped to almost a whisper. "Cut it out. You know I love you. Don't forget that."

Summer wrinkled her nose and giggled. "Okay, Super dupe."

Summer had a peculiar habit of abbreviating words. "Fab" for fabulous. "Gorge" for gorgeous. "Super dupe" for super-duper. This made her rather maddening to listen to as a weather girl, which is what Dick had tried to groom her to be.

Over a span of several years Dick had grown into the role of a quite polished Chief Meteorologist for the TV station. He sported that constant "I forgot to shave this morning" scruff that took a lot of work to maintain but women found incredibly sexy, and wore stylish suits provided for free by a local menswear shop. He was well respected even though his only study of meteorology was to check out the online weather reports and copy them word for word.

Summer had caught Dick's eye when she took a part-time job as a receptionist at the station. A late bloomer in high school, she had transformed into a blond bombshell by college age but had only begun to realize the power she held over men. She had played Audrey in *Little Shop of Horrors* at the local junior college to rave reviews, and now her heart was set on breaking into show biz. The tiny two-bit TV station seemed like the next best thing to the Great White Way.

Dick enjoyed imparting his vast television knowledge to his student, and Summer hung on his every word. He taught her to read the teleprompter without looking stiff. He taught her how to position herself in front of the green screen, which could transport the weather person to any spot on the map. He supervised her revealing wardrobe to showcase her prominent breasts.

Lance encouraged her to try her own natural personality before going into the written script. The problem was, when she tried to adlib, just about anything might blurt out of her mouth.

After a few tries that dropped like lead balloons, he strongly suggested that for her first time out she just stick to the script and keep smiling, but the young lady couldn't help herself. She debuted on the Sunday Morning News and let it fly.

"Wakey wakey, everybody, this day is going to be gorge, plus, plus!" was her opening line.

Dick cringed, but soon the phones were ringing off the hook about this beautiful new breath of fresh air.

Much of Summer's instruction took place after hours when the news set was dormant. Dick would set the camera on Summer and videotape her delivering the weather. They could then discuss her delivery and make notes. It was during these tutorials that Dick and Summer gave in to temptation. What began as flirting and a fleeting touch gave way to all-out flailing and moaning intercourse on the control room floor. Dick told himself he would keep it under control. After all, he was a married man. Two years before he had met his wife, Kristen. Not only was she attractive, she had a newspaper job that he hoped would enhance his paper-thin credibility. He was far from the poster boy for fidelity, but he at least tried to be discreet. However, when he met Summer, it turned out he had all the will power of a teenaged boy with a stack of Playboys. As for Summer, she was all-in, head over heels. She had found her Svengali and was ready to follow him anywhere.

*** 

One particular evening, after a short session of rehearsing Summer's weather delivery, they shared a bottle of cheap champagne and began to cuddle. Dick had sudden inspiration.

"You want to walk on the moon?" he said slyly.

"Walk on the moon? That's cray cray"

"Watch this."

Dick went to the switcher console and punched up a screen showing the moon's surface. The image had been used on that night's news program. "Now stand in front of the green screen," he said. Summer walked over to her usual position, looked at the monitor, and saw that she appeared to be standing on the moon.

"I'm on the fucking moon!" she squealed.

"You look good on the moon," said Dick. "Way better than Neil Armstrong. Hey, why don't you take your clothes off?"

Summer giggled and began to strip with an exaggerated bump and grind. She was soon nude on the moon. Dick Lance threw off his clothes and joined her on the set. He exclaimed in his best deep announcer voice, "This just in!"

"Super dupe!"

The revelry continued for nearly an hour, with more action than the moon had seen in its long history. With the heavy studio door locked, no one could be aware of what was going on in the newsroom. No one except for the late-night board operator who was broadcasting a vintage rerun of Gunsmoke while concentrating on a video game on his laptop. When the time came for the commercial break, the board op briefly looked up from Dungeons and Dragons to trigger a spot for a local Toyota dealer but managed to bring up the newsroom instead. Not paying attention to the monitor, Dick and Summer cavorting in the nude on the moon was broadcast to fifty thousand households.

# CHAPTER 2

Dick had already been moonlighting in the world of direct response production and voiceover work when he was abruptly fired from the TV station for his impromptu moon shot. After a few days of worrying about how he was going to continue to afford the lifestyle of a hot shot TV personality, he quickly and easily made the switch to full-time commercial production work, enticing people to pay $19.95 plus shipping and handling for each amazing new product. His moon might have eclipsed, but a new star was born.

Only one in ten direct response products actually sell well, but when they do, that $19.95 can be multiplied by millions. Summer Springfield was also dropped like a hot rock by the station. She tried to return to her quiet academic life at junior college, but snickers and sneers followed her wherever she went. She was even offered a porno movie titled, "Forecast: Hot and Steamy," but indignantly refused.

Summer finally dropped out of school; Dick kept her employed for a while with direct response commercials, demonstrating kitchen gadgets, mops, scrubbers, and pet toys, but that ended abruptly when Dick's wife Kristen laid down the law. No more Summer, period. Dick and Kristen quietly moved to the other side of town, and Dick shaved his beard.

\*\*\*

Kristen was seething. The humiliation of having her husband's nude romp televised all over the county—and then even make several late-night talk shows with discreet blurring of body parts—was simply the last slap in the face she could take. Dick had had quite the reputation as a ladies' man when she met him, but of course, she thought she could change him.

They had met at a charity dinner auction to raise money for a new fire engine. Dick was the emcee. He cut quite a figure in his pale-blue tuxedo with an outrageous ruffled shirt, a retro look, but it had been a freebie from the menswear shop that sponsored his weather segment. He handled the auction with aplomb and managed to keep the audience laughing with lame weather jokes.

Kristen was covering the event for the local newspaper's society page. When she'd graduated with a degree in journalism from Ohio State University, she'd had visions of becoming a female Woodward and Bernstein, uncovering greed and corruption, saving the planet from evildoers, and triumphantly exposing dirty politicians. Instead, she found herself reporting on fender-benders, shoplifting at Walmart, city council meetings, and covering the occasional charity function. She refrained from dating because no one in this small town was very interesting. She found the staff in the newsroom to be deadly boring except for a highly annoying sportswriter who kept hitting on her.

"Kristen Daniels with the *Gazette*," she said to Dick, extending her hand.

"I always read the *Gazette*," Dick said as he introduced himself. "It's where I steal all my weather info."

Kristen chuckled, not realizing he really meant it. The interview was light and brief, with Dick giving a few quotes about how important a new fire truck would be for the community and how he always wanted to be a firefighter. All the while he was looking her up and down like a hungry jackal. She was trim and pretty with dirty-blond hair and an engaging smile. She wore a tasteful, dark blue sleeveless cocktail dress that was quite modest compared to the bimbos he was used to dating. But it still revealed her nicely toned arms and legs. She was a refreshing change from the usual airheads and was the first woman he had met who not only was attractive enough for him to want to marry but had the credentials to help him move up in the world. As she finished jotting down notes in her notepad, he launched his best line. "How would you like to see a real TV set?"

"Um, no thanks, I've seen TV studios before," she said, thinking to herself, "At Ohio State," and wondering if a professional set was any different than the student set at the university.

Dick was flummoxed; this line was usually a real grabber. He launched into a florid description of how important meteorology was, how climate change was threatening the planet, and how much he really liked animals. Kristen was not impressed. This guy was slicker than axle grease.

The following weekend Kristen was participating in a 3K run to raise money for breast cancer awareness. Who should be handing out water bottles but Dick Lance, looking totally sporty in shorts, a polo shirt and running shoes.

"Fancy meeting you here," he said with a broad smile, offering her a cold water. "I didn't know you were a runner. Nice outfit." He ran his eyes over her shorts and T-shirt. It didn't occur to her that he had volunteered to help at a breast cancer charity to ogle breasts.

"I try to stay fit," said Kristen, caught off guard. She was impressed by his seeming interest in helping community charities—first the fire truck, now the breast cancer run. Maybe this blowhard was a good guy after all. Finally, after much talk of healthy lifestyle choices and the importance of meditation, he wore her down enough to get her phone number. And the chase was on. In a year they had married.

# CHAPTER 3

A few days after Dick wrapped up the cyclonic mop commercial, another direct-to-market operator was filming yet another new product a few hours away in Columbus, Ohio. The video production facility was hidden in an inconspicuous warehouse area near OSU. An infomercial for a new kitchen gadget had just finished taping in spectacular fashion. The crew was in a great mood, high-fiving each other, striking the set, and marveling at how seamlessly this shoot had gone. This product had actually worked!

"Congratulations, the Mega Meal A Gizer is gonna be a million seller!" said the enthusiastic director, Leon Shively, to his client, a diminutive Asian man in coat and tie by the name of Hang Foo.

"And I love the slogan, "Energize your meals with the Mega Meal A Gizer, just fantastic! That little machine is a thing of beauty!" Shively was a pot-bellied man in his late sixties with wild salt and pepper hair and regarded as one of the hottest directors in the direct response advertising business. He couldn't help but brag. "It reminds me of one of my million sellers a few years ago. You may remember it. It was called No Fakin' Bacon." His eyes widened, and his fuzzy eyebrows arched as he visualized his triumphant creation. "Crisp, tasty bacon in seconds without the greasy mess. Straight from the microwave, and cleanup's a breeze! It was seventy-five cents worth of plastic that we sold for $19.95, but the Mega Meal A Gizer. Oh, this is gonna be even bigger! Mark my words, I can feel it."

The thin, elderly man smiled broadly. "Thank you, Mr. Shively. Coming from a man of your reputation that is a fine complement. I have high hopes for this one. The elders say, 'Everything has beauty, but not everyone sees it.' My backers will be very pleased."

"Yeah, well now we've got to pick a top-notch announcer for the voiceover. I got Dick Lance to do No Fakin' Bacon. What do you think?"

Hang Foo bristled, "Dick Lance? That thief? Don't ever mention that bastard's name to me!"

Shively was caught by surprise. "Oh, you know Dick? Yeah, he does have a reputation in the business as a...well, opportunist. Good announcer, though. Don't worry, I know all the main players.

Hang Foo wrinkled his brow and studied the script.

Many direct response products have an Asian connection, being almost exclusively produced dirt cheap in either Taiwan or Hong Kong. Mr. Hang Foo, the son of immigrants, was raised in New Jersey and the first of his family to attend college. He graduated from Rutgers University with a degree in marketing and spoke Mandarin and flawless English. He got his start in advertising by working as a copy writer and proved himself worthy, but frustratingly he always seemed to be overlooked for promotion.

He began to feel discriminated against and grew tired of writing about Over Stocked Sales and Black Friday Events, turning instead to the world of direct response. A string of successful spots cemented his reputation as a winning producer. From his extensive experience, he felt that this kitchen gadget was going to be his crowning achievement, a ticket to a comfortable retirement, and using Leon Shively as director would guarantee it.

The beaming director shook his client's hand and said, "We'll be in touch when the edit is complete. Don't worry; I'll take care of everything."

Hang Foo said, "I leave it in your capable hands," gave a polite bow, and left the room.

The director's exaggerated smile gave way to a determined scowl as he stepped away from the crew, pulled out his cell phone, and began dialing. Leon Shively, a veteran of the direct response business was revered in the industry. His success rate was phenomenal, beginning with a set of kitchen knives that were guaranteed to cut through a beer can yet still slice a tomato razor-thin. There was no doubt in his mind that this kitchen gadget was going to be a huge seller.

Dick Lance answered the phone. "Hello, it's Dick."

"Dick, its's Leon Shively."

"Leon, I can't talk, I'm in the middle of recording a voiceover."

"Doesn't matter. I got a sure-fire winner, a perfect knockoff, huge seller, but it's got to be handled carefully. You interested?"

Having a total lack of scruples, Dick Lance didn't hesitate. "You bet I'm interested." He glanced over to the audio engineer and made sure his microphone wasn't hot.

"This is absolutely top secret; you can't mention it to anyone. This could make us some enemies. You need to meet me in Florida."

"I don't want to know...wait, Florida?"

"Yeah, you know, my winter place down there in Lake Worth. I can't risk carrying the prototype myself...too risky. The client's gone back to Jersey. I'm gonna get it to you tonight so you can leave tomorrow morning. I'll send it by courier; I don't want to trust it even to UPS."

"I'll book the tickets."

"No! That'll make you suspicious. They can track you. The client'll figure you took it. I think he may know you. You gotta drive."

"Don't tell me any names. But are you nuts? That'll take at least two days!"

"You gotta keep this totally secret. Don't even mention it to your wife. I'll have instructions in the package. Then I'll get the product back to the client before he suspects anything." Shively's voice dropped to an urgent note. "This is big. A sure winner! Guaranteed millions. Time is of the essence. Don't let me down." The phone fell silent.

Dick put his cell phone on mute. He put it in his pocket and stared at the script in front of him. It was for a "miracle" car polish that would give your car a showroom shine, guaranteed. He closed the door to the cramped vocal booth lined with acoustic foam and put on his headset. The director of the commercial spoke through the phones in a fed-up voice.

"Ok, this is take seven;you've got the revisions. Dick. Are you ready?"

"Yeah, but what's that smell?"

"What smell?"

Dick made an elaborate display of holding the paper to his nose at the booth window. "Oh, I know, it's the script."

"Very funny. We're rolling, anytime."

Dick Lance launched into his best deep announcer voice. He presented the "Problem" in the beginning with horrified disgust.

"Are you tired of car polishes that just don't deliver?"

Then he went on to emphasize the incredible "Magic Secret," which would be illustrated by a clip of animation to educate even the most clueless viewer.

"The secret is thousands of tiny microspheres that rejuvenate old paint like magic, bringing back its original showroom shine!"

This was followed by a series of scenes of shiny cars and supposedly ordinary folks with ecstatic smiles, who had achieved incredible results, and all for only $19.95!

"But wait!" Dick said emphatically, "If you order now, we'll DOUBLE your order That's two bottles of Righteous Ride Speedwax for the price of one if you order NOW!"

Dick finished the read and fell silent, confident that he had knocked it out of the park.

"Real good, Dick," deadpanned the director, "But we're a little long. I need you to pick up the pace and show a little extra love to the secret animation segment, ok?"

"Yeah, Bill, I get it. Speed it up but make it sound slower. I'll give it a shot, but as you know, you can't shine shit. Even with this crap."

# CHAPTER 4

Kristen Daniels never took Dick Lance's name when they married. She was too proud of her journalistic reputation. Everyone knew her byline, and frankly she had never liked the name Lance anyway.

She had a fiercely independent nature. Her policeman father taught her to defend herself, and she grew up a tomboy with the ability to intimidate any bully. In the beginning, married life was exciting and explosively romantic. Being married to a local celebrity had its benefits: better tables in restaurants, freebies from local businesses. But over time, the huckster element of Dick began to grate and the red-hot passion to fade.

The small newspaper where she worked, like so many small-town rags, began losing subscribers to social media. Advertising revenues tanked, readership dwindled, and finally the *Gazette* was sold to a large conglomerate that specialized in gobbling up failing papers.

Heads began to roll, budgets were slashed, and Kristen found herself out of a job. Even the paperboys lost their routes as the *Gazette* went from relying on print to an all-digital format.

Kristen fought back tears as she cleaned out her desk. She trudged her way to the parking lot carrying a cardboard box of sentimental memories, old notebooks, pictures, an OSU paperweight, the name plate that had sat proudly on her desk. She started her car and headed across town for Upper Arlington, the Columbus suburb where her father resided in an assisted living facility. She felt bad burdening her elderly father with her problems, but she knew that good old Dad, Tom Daniels, was the only person who could reassure her when the chips were down, as he had done so many times before.

Tom Daniels was tall, gray, and a very spry eighty-one years old. Kristen's mother had passed away three years earlier, and Arlington Oaks Assisted Living proved to be a good fit. One of the few single men there who still had his marbles, Tom was pursued relentlessly by a gaggle of lonely widows. At Christmas he was inundated with hand-knitted sweaters from his admiring harem.

Kristen took a deep breath and knocked on the door to his apartment, but when her father opened it, she couldn't help but let out a little sob. Tom Daniels gave his daughter a warm hug.

"Kristen, what's with the waterworks?"

"Oh Daddy, I lost my damn job. I just got fired."

"Hell, no. Why would they do that? You're their best writer."

"Not anymore," she sighed. "The whole paper is being downsized."

"Well, that's not the same as being fired," Tom said indignantly.

"It sure feels like it," she said with a sniff.

"Come in, come in; I'll put on some tea. Or maybe something stronger?"

As Kristen entered the familiar, tidy apartment filled with sentimental furniture from her past, the heavy weight of the situation slowly began to ease. She and her father had a long visit, reminiscing about the old days and memories of her mother. Tom had been a career policeman with a stellar reputation and was awarded a plaque upon retirement, which he proudly displayed on his living room wall next to a photo from his wedding day. Nostalgic pictures of Kristen growing up as a Girl Scout and one of her in a karate outfit were underneath. A picture of his favorite car, a 1965 Ford Mustang, hung next to an action photo of him and Kristen playing tennis.

"I miss our days playing tennis," said Kristen.

"Me too, "sighed Tom. "The assisted living watchdogs were here the other day. Wanted to take away my throw rug. Can you believe it? I've lived this long, I was a cop for over forty years, and they think a throw rug is gonna take me down."

"I'm sure they just want what's best."

The comfortable surroundings provided just the right amount of soothing that she needed. She thanked her dad for letting her lean on his shoulder. He leaned forward in his easy chair and answered with one of his favorite expressions. "Don't let the bastards get you down. You'll get through this and move on to something better. I always say it's a dumb fox that don't have two holes to his burrow." Then he shifted gears.

"What's the latest with Slick Dick?" There was no love lost between her dad and her husband.

"He's churning out irritating TV commercials one after another. Totally reinvented himself. I was amazed how he could just step into a whole new career, but I guess he's been in training for it all along."

"He's a slippery eel, that one. I don't trust that bastard at all."

"Believe me, Dad, at this point, neither do I."

When she returned home feeling sad and defeated, Dick totally blind-sided her with a pep talk. He was over-the-top enthusiastic.

"Not to worry, honey. You were wasting your time at that two-bit paper. You're a terrific writer. You can write for me. Direct response scripts. There's nothing to it. There's a formula. You grab 'em with a real catchy open that poses the "Problem," then you explain the "Magic Secret" that's gonna change their lives forever, that's "The Solution," then you give 'em the "Call To Action," so that they've gotta call right now. Not later, now! And when they do, they get a fantastic bonus absolutely free! You can help me write the script for the shoot tomorrow, we're doing a hose."

"A hose? Really?"

"Not just any hose, it's a fuckin' miracle!"

# CHAPTER 5

On a quiet tree-lined street in Upper Arlington, Dick had reserved a grand, three-bedroom two-bath home complete with a pool and hot tub through VRBO. Although he had said on the contract that this would be a relaxing weekend getaway for the family, a grip truck full of cameras and equipment showed up early Saturday morning. Electricians readied lights and reflectors in the backyard.

An audio man awkwardly ran a lavalier microphone under the shirt of a model named Verushka, Dick Lance's latest find. She was a Russian photography model who could barely speak English, which didn't matter at all because there was no dialogue except for "Wow" and "Amazing!" Her main qualification for this shoot, aside from her looks, was being someone other than Summer Springfield.

The hose product was guaranteed to never kink and to last a lifetime. It was called the Anaconda King 2000. No one ever questioned why the number 2000 was used, but it just seemed so splashy. When the water was turned on the hose would triple in size. The new script written by Kristen seemed like a winner to Dick. His wife had totally new twists on the shop-worn phrases, "Guaranteed to change your life," and "But wait! There's more!" This business partnership might just breathe new life into their bedroom, too, he thought.

"Okay, just a few establishing shots," said Dick. "Camera, action. Verushka, honey, turn on the water and hold up the hose to the camera."

Verushka stared blankly. She didn't have a clue, but she looked stunning in short shorts and sneakers with a striped sailor top. Dick pantomimed how to turn on the hose, and she bent over the spigot with a grand flourish and cranked the water on full blast, causing the Anaconda to swell in size like a clown balloon. It jerked out of her hand and sprayed the crew with a torrent of water, bucking and coiling like a live snake.

"Amazing!" she exclaimed.

"Cut. All right, that was a learning experience. Let's go again."

Recording settled into an easy pace. The intro was of an

old, tangled hose that could have been from World War II, with an obvious gushing leak. A big red X would appear over this horrible abomination. Then, Verushka introduced the "Solution," the amazing Anaconda King 2000! She sprinkled bushes effortlessly, sprayed windows with aplomb, and washed the family car in no time. All with no kinks!

From across the street, Noreen Fremont peered out her second-floor window, fuming. This illegal rental house had been used for loud drunken frat parties in the past, usually leaving the neighborhood awash in beer bottles and pizza boxes. When the grip truck showed up and the technicians began their setup, Noreen called the cops.

The final demonstration shot of the incredible strength of the Anaconda was to use it as a tow rope to pull a pickup truck. A burly tow truck driver with a lumberjack beard fastened one end of the hose to his tow truck and the other end to the front bumper of the pickup. He gave an enthusiastic thumbs up to the camera and got in his truck.

Totally dominating this quiet street with lights, reflectors and camera gear, the crew held their breath as the tow truck revved up. A zoomed-in close-up on the hose showed it was easily taking the strain. The pickup truck began to roll triumphantly down the street; then, suddenly sirens blared, and a police car roared up to shut the whole shoot down.

Naturally, Dick Lance had not obtained a permit for this production in a quiet residential neighborhood. Permits cost money. He did some fast talking, was given a citation, and told to cease and desist. He let out a deep breath, thankful he had talked Kristen out of joining him at the shoot this morning. This was a side of his business he wasn't ready to give up. The after-party. If Kristen had come, his usual after-shoot celebration with the female talent would be more than a bit awkward. It was a win-win all around, Dick decided.

"Wow," said Verushka, confused.

"Don't worry, we've got plenty of footage to make this work. That's a wrap, guys! Be careful on your way out, I want my deposit back on this joint. Hey Verushka, you were great!"

The crew broke down their equipment and loaded it into their truck under the watchful eye of the policeman while Noreen Fremont stared triumphantly out her window. Dick and Verushka retreated into the rental home where they made good use of the hot tub.

# CHAPTER 6

Kristen's script writing turned out to be among the best in the business. She quickly adapted her writing style to be punchy, direct, and not too dependent on the pesky rules of grammar. She cleverly rhymed words for maximum impact. "Is housework a chore? Not anymore!"

This new writing outlet gave her bruised ego a boost. At least she could feel in her heart that she was still a writer and using her journalism degree. Somewhat. She kept her hand in as a regular contributor of letters to the editor at the *Columbus Dispatch*, mostly on the subject of climate change, which her husband didn't care a fig about.

But, as the months went by and Kristen learned more and more about Dick's business, she began to realize that her husband was spending an inordinate amount of time away from the office without any legitimate reason. He seemed to have an inordinate number of lengthy "meetings" and spent a ridiculous amount of time doing "research" and scouting "new products" at trade shows that would take him away for days while racking up enormous hotel bills. All of this could be optimistically overlooked without any actual proof of infidelity.

Wishful thinking is the easiest thinking of all. But she could never wish away the infamous Moon Caper. The stinging humiliation of the moon sex catastrophe was more than any marriage could survive, and Kristen had been looking for an exit strategy to leave this pompous jerk for months.

\*\*\*

Kristen was sitting in her home office one afternoon, searching for rhyming words to describe a new cooker. "Now, take your meals from tragic, to magic!" No, too much. "Take your meals from ho-hum to yum yum!" No, too corny. "Is your dinner a joke 'cause your guests start to choke? Not anymore!" Pathetic. She stared at her computer and wondered where Dick was this time. He was late, but she was used to that. Suddenly he burst into her office.

"We have to drive to Florida. Immediately!"

"What? Did you hit a Happy Hour again?" Kristen tried to brush him off before she forgot her rhyme and had to start over. Then the words sank in.

"You must be out of your mind." She rolled her eyes. "Drive to Florida?"

"The opportunity of a lifetime!" he insisted. "Seriously, you have no idea what this could mean to our future. And we'll see some sights."

"What future, asshole?" she thought, ruefully. But he was insistent, and since she had no steady job to go to anyway, they loaded a few bags into their trusty Dodge minivan and headed south early the next morning.

The first night of the journey they stayed in one of Dick's favorite memories from his youth, South of the Border, a quirky roadside attraction off I-95 just south of the divide between North and South Carolina. The sprawling beacon of highway kitsch was hard to miss. A giant statue of the sombrero-wearing mascot Pedro still welcomed weary travelers into a fantasy land, just as Dick remembered. Plastic dinosaurs, pink deer, a huge gorilla, and other family-friendly photo-op creatures were distributed randomly around the grounds of the hotel/miniature golf course/funky tourist magnet. At check-in, Kristen requested two beds instead of one, causing Dick to bite his lip in frustration. His hopes for make-up sex had just gone right out the window, but he wasn't about to start an argument. It was much more important to get the Mega Meal A Gizer to Florida. He would be on his best behavior, deliver the prototype to Shively, then sweet talk his angry wife into a night of Viagra-fueled passion. Dick challenged Kristen to a game of putt-putt golf, which she won handily even though she caught Dick trying to cheat by nudging his ball with his foot.

"Only you would try to cheat at miniature golf," she said.

"Best two out of three," he whined.

"Don't be a sore loser," she chided.

Dick dejectedly had a few cocktails at the bar to wash down his defeat. They ate a spicy taco dinner special with cold beers, which gave Dick heartburn. The next morning, they got an early start, but he couldn't help buying a bag of over-priced fireworks for old times' sake.

\*\*\*

The first night was bad; but the second night was total disaster. A little past midnight, in a Florida no-man's land, Dick and Kristen were trudging on foot along the highway. The night was dark as a cave. Crickets and frogs creaked and croaked, making unworldly sounds that conjured up goblins and ghouls. A mixture of decaying swamp odors and fertilizer wafted on a humid wind, making Kristen want to gag. She stumbled on the cracked two-lane road for the fifth time, nearly falling. She became shocked at herself as she suddenly realized this would be a great time to kill her husband.

Out here in the middle of nowhere.

The minivan they were driving had suddenly and inexplicably stopped. No cell phone coverage. No civilization in sight. Just miles and miles of acrid swamp and sugarcane.

This lonely portion of Highway 441 east of Lake Okeechobee is paralleled by a deep canal, a vestige of the Army Corps of Engineers' ambitious program to drain and tame the Everglades. These canals regularly swallow up cars, trucks, motorcycles, pets, and people. Usually by accident, but every now and then, definitely on purpose. Whoops! Splash. Goodbye.

Dick Lance, raised in Chillicothe, Ohio, where the biggest body of water was the municipal swimming pool, was a horrible swimmer. Even more so with a half-bottle of Stolichnaya under his belt, as he had right now.

"Slow down, Dick," said Kristin, "I didn't bring my walking shoes."

"Of course not," slurred Dick. "You only have a pair for every day of the year. What's the matter with those dogs?"

"You told me it was just around the bend."

"That's what the damn sign said. You saw it, 'Last Chance Gas, five hundred yards.' Just like the South of the Border signs with Pedro."

Kristin smacked a mosquito from her face. "This is absolutely the stupidest thing you've ever done, Dick."

"Shut up, Kristen, you're not helping."

Dick had decided against taking I-95 all the way because he wanted to relive his youth when his parents made driving trips with the whole family from Ohio through the center of

Florida. This turned out to be a terrible idea that ate up a lot of time. He tried to point out his favorite roadside attractions to Kristen, but most had been bulldozed long ago. Kristen was doing a slow burn. She told him this route was a mistake, but as usual, he didn't listen. If he hadn't been so pig-headed, they could have sped down I-95 or the Florida Turnpike and been at Leon's place down in Lake Worth hours ago, putting their feet up and having a cocktail. When he realized the night was dragging on and they weren't making good progress, he asked his cell phone to find a short cut to the coast. A few miles down this dark deserted road, cell phone coverage abruptly stopped. And then the minivan had followed suit.

Dick and Kristen trudged down the road serenaded by the song of the swamp. The chirping of frogs, the whine of mosquitoes and the occasional grunt of an alligator sang through the muggy night. What they didn't know was that no one had ever measured the distance boldly promised on those signs. The proprietor, Billy Strongbow, had simply pulled them out of thin air. "Bloodthirsty alligators! Last Chance, GAS! 10 miles ahead!" "Airboat rides! Last Chance GAS! 8 miles ahead!" "Hungry? Put some South in your mouth! Last Chance GAS! 5 miles." "Petting zoo! Alligator wrestling! Good grub! Last Chance GAS! 3 miles!" They trudged on, like moths to a flame.

"We should've just waited in the car," snarled Kristin, "At least we wouldn't be eaten alive by these damn mosquitoes!"

"Not bothering me," Dick lied.

Dick and Kristin had settled into the back and forth no-give all-take of broken-marriage feuding. They tramped on in silence for another moment. Dick stared straight ahead down the narrow empty road.

"Where the fuck is it?"

Dick resolved that once he reached civilization, he would just rent a car, any car, and get out for good. Bang. Just like that. Kristen could deal with the busted minivan. He just wanted out, right now.

Business was booming. He would finally start spending his money and live like a rock star. Get a flashy apartment, maybe buy a Porsche. That would be great. A real chick magnet. No more "Dick, do this," or "Dick, do that." He'd really live it up. This was an epiphany. All his murky plans for the future suddenly became as clear as a glass of Stoli. Dick stopped in his tracks.

"That's IT." he said firmly.

"That's what?"

"The end of the line, Kristen." He glared at her in the darkness. She stared back. He would have told her more. A lot more. He would have told her about the trysts with a makeup artist in a broom closet that lasted for three months until she wanted a commitment, and he had her fired. He would have told her about the occasional blowjob from his ex- best friend's ex-wife when she had a little too much to drink. And he would have told her about the glorious yet cramped sex he'd had with a complete stranger on a red-eye flight from LA in the aircraft lavatory. And, oh, what he could tell her about Summer! Hah! He would have told her all these things and a lot more, except as he was about to speak, he noticed headlights approaching them from behind.

"Shit! It's a car! We can get a ride!"

They watched transfixed as the headlights grew larger and the sound of a Ford Econoline van with a bad muffler became audible. It grew like a mirage from the swampy horizon. The van swerved slightly from side to side. Dick flapped his arms wildly to flag it down. "Over here!" he shouted, leaning toward the centerline.

The impact of the right front bumper spun Dick around like a roulette wheel, arms flailing, one of which caught Kristen square on the jaw with a powerful upper cut, knocking her over. There was nothing to stop Dick's lurching flight over the bank and into the canal where he landed with a huge splash, sinking immediately. Silence returned to the dark stretch of the highway as the taillights of the speeding Econoline disappeared down the road.

\*\*\*

Armando Ramirez had barely felt a thing through the

wheel of his Ford van, which had a bad shimmy anyway. He had been looking down between his legs, fishing for a boiled peanut that had fallen under his crotch. The steady, throbbing racket of the busted muffler drowned out any possibility of hearing Dick's shouts. That strange little bump could have been an opossum, raccoon, gopher turtle, or maybe something that was already dead. He checked his rearview mirror and saw nothing. Armando had a whole car full of illegal immigrant pole bean pickers that needed to get back to the migrant workers camp before they were missed. Eight people, mostly Mexican, were packed into the old Econoline, and all eight were fast asleep. Armando himself was nearly asleep at the wheel, but that's what comes from working all day in a bean field under the hot Florida sun.

\*\*\*

Many minutes later, Kristen raised her head from the side of the road. She was completely disoriented, covered in dirt, and totally alone. No sign of Dick, no sign of the van that had hit him. Crickets and frogs kept up their relentless song. Her jaw ached; her shoulder throbbed.

"Dick?" she called timidly, then louder, knowing in her heart that there would be no answer. She slowly got to her feet and stood at the canal edge, staring into the inky blackness of the calm water in a daze. Her stomach was in knots. She stood there for many moments, trembling, not knowing what to do. Try to find the body in the water? The thought sent shivers down her spine. Stay there to wait for help? The buzz of mosquitoes and the chorus of the frogs seemed to settle the issue.

"I'm sorry," she cried, sobbing, tears flowing, hot burning guilt searing her mind at the thought of wishing her husband dead just moments before. She sobbed by the bank of the canal for what seemed like an eternity; then, she said a prayer for Dick and slowly resumed walking down the desolate road. Within minutes, a faint glow appeared on the horizon like a luminescent fog. A gaudy neon sign that read, "LAST CHANCE, GAS!"

# CHAPTER 7

Kristen stumbled numbly into the parking lot of The Alligator Outpost. It was eerily quiet. After seeing so many large, boasting billboards, Kristen was surprised at the tiny size of the place. A set of gas pumps, a small cafe, gift shop, and general store with an aging building marked "office," and two rows of faux Indian teepees made of concrete which served as guest lodgings. There were signs everywhere. "Gifts," "Beer," "Souvenirs," "Alligator Wrestling Daily," "Airboat Rides." The place had obviously been there a long time, and everything she saw was in need of a coat of paint.

The Everglades Outpost was just one of dozens of Florida tourist attractions that struggled for survival after the Florida Turnpike and I-95 bypassed the smaller roads. The opening of Disney World drove a stake through the heart of these mom-and-pop establishments, and they began to die one by one, to be replaced with condo developments, strip malls, tattoo parlors, and used car lots.

Billy Strongbow retaliated with his elaborate series of billboards which promised everything from the best night's sleep to the world's best catfish and hush puppies, to the coldest beer on the planet, and of course the "Last Chance Gas" before crossing an immense stretch of swampland that would challenge the ability of any vehicle. In reality, the nearest gas stop was only fifteen miles away, an inconvenient fact not mentioned in any of Billy's signs.

Kristen approached the office. Everything was dark despite the signs on the road proclaiming "Open 24 hours!" She found a little button marked "Night Service" by the door and pressed it. A tiny buzzer sounded, then nothing.

She waited, pressed the buzzer again. Still nothing. "Hello?" she called. Just as Kristen was about to pound on the door, it swung open. A short, gray-haired elderly woman of Native American descent wearing a bathrobe and moccasins appeared in the doorway. "How can I help you?"

Kristen poured out her story through a stream of tears. The car breaking down, the long walk down the road, the hit-and-run driver, and the disappearance of her husband into the opaque drainage canal.

"Oh, you poor thing," the woman gasped. "I'll call the sheriff for you. Let's get you a room so you can rest. Oh, my, would you like something to drink?"

The tiny woman grabbed a key from a row of hooks on the wall and showed Kristen to a teepee marked "Fox." All of the teepees had animal names: Bear, Gator, Panther, Eagle, Bobcat, Hawk, and Moose. Kristen didn't bother to wonder why moose happened to be in this collection of Florida creatures. In truth, teepees were just as out of place as moose in Florida. She was glad to have a place to lie down. The concrete teepee was actually quite comfortable, with a whirring window air conditioning unit, a double bed, a chest of drawers, TV, phone, and writing table. A far cry from the real thing.

Kristen splashed water on her face and looked at herself in the mirror. She was a mess. Dirt and twigs on her clothing. Mascara running down her cheeks, hair going every which way, and a hideous black-and-blue shiner circling her right eye where her husband's flailing arm had socked her on his way to his late-night swim. She used a washcloth to clean her face, then ran cold water on the cloth and pressed it gingerly to her swollen eye. She sat on the bed wondering what to do next. She was tired, but there was no way she could sleep now.

\*\*\*

Sheriff's deputy Mike Russell had just pointed his patrol car toward home when the call came over the radio. "Russell, we got a hit-and-run out on 441 about a mile north of Alligator Outpost."

"Holy crap," sighed Russell before keying the microphone, "C'mon, man, can't you get anyone else to cover it? My shift ends in ten minutes."

"No can do," came the reply. "Samuels is busy with a fender bender on Southern Boulevard, Cooper's got a B and E in Belle Glade, and Lawrence has his hands full takin' a bunch of spring breakers to the lockup. They were buck naked swimmin' in the fountain at the Hilton. You're it."

"Roger that, EMT on the way?"

"No rush, the victim's sleepin' with the fishes. Lady at the Outpost said he went into the canal."

"I should be there in about thirty minutes," Russell said wearily as he hit the lights and siren, whipped his car across the median in a hard U-turn and headed west.

Law enforcement coverage is almost nonexistent in the remote areas of Palm Beach County. The county is one of the largest in the state, stretching from the swamps of the Everglades to the posh palaces of the coast. Mike Russell pressed the accelerator down, and the patrol car hurtled through the night.

This was yet another in a string of late-night calamities that made Russell want to change careers. He had been enjoying a higher rank and better pay until a deadly shootout with a child pornographer was ruled excessive force. Russell had no regrets, but now he was stuck with the late-night shit patrol. Just when he thought he was about to get back to his tidy little house in Lake Worth, this happened. It would be hours before he could sleep. He hoped his dog, Rocket, a middle-aged rescue dog of dubious heritage, wouldn't crap on the floor. He always looked so guilty when that happened.

\*\*\*

Kristen had been dreading the knock on the door of her teepee. She opened it to find Sheriff's Deputy Russell, tall, physically fit, wearing a dark green uniform with clipboard in hand, looking sleepy. Kristen invited him in and began to explain the terrible circumstances of her evening all over again.

Deputy Russell was efficient and perfunctory, yet sympathetic to this woman's plight. He had a lot of experience in calming the nerves of accident victims, and he spoke in a soft reassuring tone to Kristen. He asked her if she was up to taking a ride back down the highway to the scene of the accident.

"I…I guess so," replied Kristen. "I don't think I can possibly sleep now anyway."

"I understand," said Russell soothingly. "I won't keep you any longer than necessary."

They drove up the dark road in silence except for the

occasional crackle of the patrol car's radio.

"My father was a cop," Kristen said, staring ahead into the blackness.

"Oh really?"

"Yup. Still keeps a sidearm hidden in the nightstand at his old folks' home. He taught me to shoot when I was fourteen. So, I know what your life can be like. He put in long hours and never made a lot of money, but he's a good man. A good father."

"Something I aspire to."

"Which, good man or good father?"

"Both. I guess I'll take it one at a time."

In just a few minutes the abandoned Dodge minivan came into view. The distance had seemed so much longer when Kristen was slogging on foot.

"Any idea what's wrong with the car?" asked Russell.

"Not the foggiest. It just started to sputter and buck. I thought my brilliant husband might have let it run out of gas, but he swore he had a quarter of a tank."

"Well, we'll have it towed and checked out."

"Towed to where?" asked Kristen.

"The place where you're staying. They've got a tow truck and a garage for minor repairs. Didn't you see all those screwy signs?"

"How could we not? They're everywhere, and they're eyesores."

"That's the work of Chief Billy Strongbow; he's the brains behind that cuckoo's nest." Russell pulled to a stop and picked up a big flashlight.

"You're saying it's a nuthouse?"

Deputy Russell rolled his eyes. "We never know what kind of shit show we're going to step into out there. Everything from typical domestic disturbances, you know, husbands and wives duking it out in those 'authentic' teepees, to drunks, to rattlesnake bites. We even had to come out once when old Billy got his freakin' finger bit off by an alligator."

"What?" gasped Kristen.

"Well, he was wrestling it at the time. Funny thing is, we had to shoot the gator with a tranquilizer because he wouldn't let us kill it. Damned if he didn't reach into that gator's mouth and get his finger back. He wears it on a little leather thong around his neck. Oh, you'll see all kinds of bizarre stuff there by the light of day. I mean, I assume you'll be there awhile."

"At least until the car is fixed," she sighed.

"You wait here," said Russell as he snapped the flashlight on and got out. He made his way carefully through the low weeds to the bank of the canal, sweeping the powerful light back and forth. No sign of life and no sign of death, just inky black water. He pointed the light farther down the canal and saw the unmistakable reflection of a pair of alligator eyes, glowing red, watching silently. He turned and trained the light on the Dodge, then walked back to the patrol car.

"Nothing. We'll have divers out first thing in the morning. Shouldn't take long. Our guys have a lot of experience at this, unfortunately."

"Well, wait a minute. He didn't go in the water here. It was about a half mile down the road."

"Oh. Of course." He gave an exasperated sigh. "Well, that widens the area of interest. You need to get anything else out of the car?"

Kristen got out of the patrol car and opened the door to the van. An empty Stolichnaya bottle clanked to the ground at her feet.

"Doing a little imbibing?"

"Not me, that was all Dick. He never went anywhere without his vitamin V, his vodka."

"Was he drunk tonight?"

"Well, that's hard to say, but most likely. He had a ridiculously high tolerance. He was proud of how much he could drink and still drive."

"An accident waiting to happen."

"Yeah, I hated his drinking. It's ironic that he went the way he did…just walking down the road. If only we'd walked a little farther." Russell shined the flashlight through the car as Kristen retrieved her suitcase.

"Looks like a bag of fireworks."

"Oops, that's Dick again. He could never resist a

fireworks stand. Just a big kid that way. We bought them at South of the Border."

"Great place, South of the Border. Used to stop there when I was a kid. Kind of run down now."

"Tell me about it," Kristen said sarcastically.

"Well, I'll have to confiscate the fireworks. Illegal, y'know. Confidentially, I'm partial to bottle rockets. So, you hated his drinking, eh?" asked Russell, hefting the South of the Border bag. "Did you fight about it? I couldn't help but notice that nasty Mike Tyson shiner."

"Well, that was an accident. That van hit so hard. But, yeah, we fought constantly. I don't know why he couldn't be happy without booze. I would always wonder, am I talking to the real Dick or the drunk Dick?"

"I'm sure many women have asked that question," Russell said dryly.

# CHAPTER 8

The next morning Kristen awoke with a start. She had been dreaming about her husband, who was doing the backstroke in a deep black canal.

"Come on in, the water's fine!" he called. "What are ya', chicken?" He squirted a mouthful of canal water into the air like a fountain, swimming in circles.

She rubbed her eyes and looked at the clock on the nightstand. 9:30 a.m. Kristen had slept a lot longer than she intended. She quickly freshened up and ventured outside.

Under the bright Florida sun, the Alligator Outpost looked more faded and forlorn than ever. She walked across the dusty courtyard and opened the door to the cafe. Inside, the hodgepodge of bric-a-brac, souvenirs, stuffed animals, and downright useless crap was overwhelming. One counter had a row of bleached alligator skulls and varnished baby gators with perpetually frozen, toothy smiles. Another displayed coconuts carved in the shape of goofy heads. On a rack in the corner stood a collection of magic tricks, itching powder, stink bombs, rubber vomit, and dog poo.

"How did you sleep, dear?" called a voice from behind the lunch counter.

It was the little old Native American lady who had greeted Kristen at the office door the night before.

"Actually, better than I expected," she answered. "Thanks so much for your help."

"Don't worry about a thing; you're with Mama now. That's what everyone calls me. Coffee?"

"Please." Kristen took a seat at the deserted lunch counter. Mama poured a cup of coffee while humming a sweet, nameless tune and wiped her hands on a colorful handmade apron. Her dark eyes twinkled from a delicate framework of wrinkles that lined her brown face.

"So, are you a Seminole?" asked Kristen.

"Nope, not a Miccosukee either," she said in a soft, high voice and laughed. "You'll never guess my tribe. I'm pretty much the last of the line, too. The last of the Mohicans...if I was a Mohican. My people are known as the Hingahong. It means Music People."

"I don't think I've ever heard of that tribe."

"Not surprised. They've all died off or scattered to the winds. I've got a cousin in Indianapolis. I always thought that was a funny name for a town. What would you like for breakfast?"

"Nothing really, "answered Kristen. "I don't have much of an appetite. Very good coffee, though."

At that moment a family of four burst through the door. Two elementary school age boys ran to the alligator skulls and shouted, "Dinosaurs!" The haggard husband and wife looked as though they had been on the road for an eternity. They disappeared into the restrooms labeled Braves and Squaws and emerged moments later. "Let's make this quick," barked the father.

"Excuse me a minute," said Mama to Kristen as she stepped out from behind the lunch counter to greet the family and ring up their purchases.

Suddenly, the sharp crack of a whip snapped through the air like a firecracker as a tall aging man in full Indian headdress and buckskins materialized at the back of the gift shop. He appeared to be right out of a spaghetti western.

"Palefaces!" shouted the imposing Indian with a toothy smile, gesturing wildly. "Palefaces, come see-um alligator wrestling!"

"Wah!" screamed the two little boys.

"Jeez, you scared the shit out of my kids!" snapped the father as the boys ran to hide behind their mom.

"Oh, uh, me heap sorry."

"Bill! I told you not to crack that whip in the store; it's too loud!" scolded Mama.

"Sorry," said the chief in a tone that said he'd like to slap those kids silly. "So, you folks want to see gator wrestling? How about an airboat ride?"

"I don't think so, Tonto," sneered the father as he paid for a box of peanut brittle and some Cokes. "We're outta here." The door slammed as the family rushed outside.

Mama let out a sigh, "Bill…"

"I know, I know. I came on a little strong. Hey, we need

the business," Billy Strongbow said dejectedly. He turned and looked at Kristen and gave her a warm smile. "Hey, little lady, how are you doing this morning?"

"I've been better," offered Kristen.

"I understand. Heap sorry, I mean, very sorry about your loss. Just so you know, your car was towed here, and it's up on the lift right now. We should know more about what's wrong with it before too long. We've got our boy Joe on it. He's a whiz with cars." The big man sidled up to the tiny woman and gave her a squeeze. "I see you've met the missus."

"I have. So, you're a member of the Hingahong tribe, too?"

"Me? Well, kind of an honorary member," he said vaguely. "I'm from a totally different tribe in upstate New York."

"Bill, why don't you do something useful and go help Joe, and try not to scare away the customers," said Mama, giving him a nudge.

"All right," he replied, returning to his tourist lingo. "Me hitting dusty dangerous trail." And with that he was gone through the back entrance. A whipcrack sounded in the distance.

Kristen finished her coffee and found herself staring at the empty cup, wondering what the day would bring. Mama noticed her blank expression.

"I know you need a lot of time for healing, my dear. If you'd like to take your mind off all this terrible news, you might want to come with me out to the petting zoo. It's feeding time, and I could use a little help."

Kristen brightened. "That sounds like a great idea!"

Mama led Kristen out of the Outpost Cafe and down a curving, narrow brick path that ended under a towering live oak tree. Spanish moss hung from the branches like a grand lady's gray shawl, gently swaying in the breeze.

"What a magnificent tree," marveled Kristen.

"They called this the Meeting Tree. Been here forever. Tribes would meet here to hash out differences, trade goods, and swap stories. This is actually considered sacred ground by the elders."

Beneath the tree's sheltering arms, a cluster of pens and cages were arranged in the shade. Chickens pecked at the ground in one pen; a pair of white rabbits with wiggling noses stared expectantly from another. Two little lambs bleated excitedly from behind a wire fence in anticipation of mealtime.

"Everybody, wait your turn," chided Mama. "Here Kristen, why don't you feed some bunny chow to Anthony and Cleopatra."

Kristen filled the rabbits' bowl and replenished their water dish. Mama broke off some leaves of lettuce for the rabbits, then placed the rest on the ground of a pen that appeared empty. Slowly, a large turtle the size of a bowling ball made its way out of a wooden shelter and moved toward the lettuce, awkwardly dragging a hind leg.

"Got hit by a car," said Mama. "He's already gotten a lot better. They call 'em gopher turtles. They're indigenous. Dig deep burrows. This one should have stayed in his hole. We call him Lucky. Lots of our animals are rescue critters. When people can't care for them, or they get hurt, we give 'em a home. Here's a fine example. One of my favorites."

Mama approached a large cage with a sizeable hawk in it. Its sharp talons were wrapped around a wooden perch; its black, piercing eyes and curved, sharp beak gave it a fierce demeanor, but its right wing could not fold normally.

"Another car hit," said Mama softly. "Probably swooped down on a critter in the road. Maybe a mouse. Maybe a bunny," she said glancing over at Anthony and Cleopatra contentedly munching away. "The vet looked him over, and he thinks he'll make it."

"Beautiful feathers," said Kristen, "But kind of a mean face."

"Oh yeah, red-tailed hawk. They dive down on their prey and grab 'em in those sharp talons. Interestingly, they're monogamous. I've seen his mate fly overhead here from time to time. Probably wonders what's going on. Don't you worry, Red; you'll be back with your sweetie real soon." She aimed the last remark at the hawk, who gazed hungrily at his breakfast.

Kristen and the tiny Indian woman went from cage to cage until the whole menagerie was cared for. It was the most relaxed Kristen had been in a long time.

# CHAPTER 9

Back in West Palm Beach, Deputy Mike Russell had been doing some digging into the background of the missing and presumed deceased Dick Lance. He discovered that Lance was quite a successful producer of direct-response TV commercials, those seemingly endless spots for exercise machines, diet pills, kitchen gadgets and beauty products that promise to change your life for only $19.95 (If you order now!) Russell remembered the one time he had actually bought one of those TV products, "the Egger Gizer," a microwave omelet maker that had exploded in his microwave creating a sticky, gooey mess.

Russell placed a call to Dick Lance's company, Lance Direct, Inc., but only got a recording. The phone message suggested visiting the company's website at LanceDirect.com, so he did. The website homepage featured a smiling Dick Lance surrounded by a table full of gadgets he had promoted on TV. Sure enough, one of the items was the Egger Gizer. "Sonofabitch" he muttered. Clicking on a particular product opened a description of the item. Russell learned about Fix-O-2000, a miracle glue that was so strong you could glue freight cars together.

Pet Polish promised to destroy embarrassing pet odors or your money back and Let Freedom Roll was a musical toilet roll holder that played the *Star-Spangled Banner*. Russell didn't bother clicking on the Egger Gizer.

"Doing a little online shopping?" asked Captain Block, stepping into the room and eyeing the computer. He was a beefy, silver-haired man with a bushy mustache and sagging eyelids that made him look perpetually sad. As a boss he was old-school law enforcement with little sense of humor.

"Just getting a little background on that canal floater. Looks like he may have been a pretty successful guy. May be worth some decent dough," said Russell.

"So, you think the grieving widow might have given him a little shove to collect on an insurance policy?"

"Maybe. She doesn't seem like the type, but who knows? Money does weird things to people. She did get a mean shiner on the night in question."

"Love tap, huh? At this point we don't have squat," sighed the captain. "In addition to which, we still don't have a suspect vehicle, assuming it exists. Maybe you should look a little further into the lady's background, check out assets, bank accounts, the usual."

Mike Russell shut down the computer and straightened up the desk. He'd been afraid this might happen. More tedious paperwork. Another boring drive all the way out into the boonies to Billy Strongbow's Alligator Outpost. Why couldn't this be a nice, neat, open-and-shut case complete with a dented car, a remorseful driver, and best of all, a corpse?

Russell thought about Kristen. What was she really like? She seemed nice enough, but he knew from bitter experience that you can't judge a book by its cover or a woman by her appearance. His failed marriage, which had ended after only three years, had schooled him on that. His wife had been everything he had ever hoped for. Attractive, athletic, terrific lover. She was the perfect mate, except for an annoyingly shrill voice and a worrisome prescription pill habit.

He was blindsided by the breakup. She left him for an Elvis impersonator she had met in a karaoke lounge. Mike hated karaoke. When his wife had a couple of drinks under her belt she would get up and sing *We Are Family*, much to his embarrassment.

He later realized that her repeated requests for *"Hunka hunka burnin' love"* from the faux Elvis might have been a tipoff. Perhaps she had more in common with Elvis in his later years than she did with a sheriff's deputy who spent long hours away from home and didn't much care for nightlife. Mike never gave a thought about remarrying. He didn't have any patience for the dating scene and felt that online dating was just plain weird. To not have started a family made him feel like a failure, but Rocket, the composite dog, was company enough for him. He was confident that the dog wouldn't leave him for anyone in show business.

\*\*\*

"It's the brain," said Joe, squinting from under the hood

of Kristen's minivan. "The brain?" she asked, puzzled.

"Yeah, all these cars these days have a brain, you know, that controls everything. It looks like you'll be needing a new brain."

"Just like Monty Python," she said. Joe looked quizzical.

"You know, the TV show. It looks like you'll be needing a new brain."

"I'm not familiar with that, ma'am," said Joe. She looked him over and wondered how this handsome young man could be related to the Indian couple.

He certainly didn't look Native American, with longish blond hair and blue eyes. He was tall and fairly muscular, and he looked more German than anything else. She guessed him to be mid to late twenties.

"Anyways, we can go ahead and order the new brain. It may take a day or two to get here. Everything takes a little longer to get when you are out here in the sticks."

"Yes, well, go ahead and order it. Let's get this sucker fixed," said Kristen. "Is there a rental car place around here?"

"No ma'am, but there's really no place to go anyway, unless you want to go into West Palm. That's pretty much the big city for us. They've got a Walmart."

"Do you get to the city much?"

"Shucks no, ma'am. I've got a lot to do here at the Outpost. There's always a car that needs fixin', animals need feedin', the floors need sweepin'.

"You can't just work all the time," said Kristen, trying to imagine being stuck in this forlorn enclave day in and day out. Joe looked down at the floor with a hint of embarrassment.

"Well, I do artwork for fun. It's not much." "You mean Indian crafts?" she asked.

"No, the real Indians do those. I make paintings. Maybe you saw them over in the store."

Kristen thought for a moment. "I don't recall seeing any paintings, and what do you mean by real Indians?"

Joe wiped his greasy fingers with a rag. "I'm only half Indian. Billy's not my dad. But he does treat me like a son. Most of the time, anyhow. I never knew my real dad. Mama gave me a new name when he left. Glades. I'm Joe Glades. You know, like the Everglades. I guess my dad left Mama when I was really little."

"I'm sorry to hear that," said Kristen. "I shouldn't be so nosey."

"Ain't no biggie," said Joe with a shrug, "So, you wanna see my paintings?

"I'd love to."

Joe Glades led her across the hot parking lot to a side door of the gift shop she hadn't noticed before. The air was cool inside and the lighting dim, which helped accentuate the many canvases up on the wall. Each was lit individually with an overhead light.

"Oh. Oh my," said Kristen, not wishing to convey her astonishment at seeing so many paintings on velvet displayed in such a reverential manner. There was a large painting of dogs playing poker. A panther stalking through the Everglades. An American eagle with an American flag in the background. A bare-breasted Indian maiden holding a plate of corn. A triple portrait of JFK, RFK, and Martin Luther King. And in a place of honor on an easel with a spotlight shining brightly from the ceiling, a portrait of Elvis in his prime, with his trademark sneer.

"Wow," she managed. "That's something."

"Thanks," Joe answered modestly. "People seem to like 'em a lot. We sell quite a few. Mama says she's gonna put all the money in one of those trusts for me. You know, for the future."

"And what do you want to do in the future?"

"Gee, I don't know, but I guess it couldn't hurt to have a little saved up for something."

"Well, best of luck to you. Maybe you'll become a famous artist," she offered.

"I doubt that," said Joe shyly." I ain't doin' anything nobody else isn't doin'."

Kristen walked over to examine more closely a painting on velvet of Ronald Reagan at the Alamo. It really was a pretty good likeness of the old Gipper. She was reminded of what her husband Dick had said, "There's a market for just about anything."

It was then that she noticed more canvases stacked behind Reagan's Alamo triumph. She lifted the Reagan painting and revealed another painting, not on velvet, but canvas. And not a portrait cliche, but a stunning abstract. Vivid swirls of color in bold, clashing strokes seemed to jump from the surface. Kristen couldn't take her eyes off it.

"That ain't nothin," said Joe apologetically, "that's just foolin' around."

"You painted this, Joe? It's fantastic!" she exclaimed. Joe said nothing, seeming to be totally embarrassed.

"No really," continued Kristen, "this says something. Do you have more of these?"

"Just a few, but nobody wants to see those."

"How do you know? Have you ever displayed them?"

"Nope. Not really, no." He gulped with embarrassment, staring at the floor.

She found more abstract canvases hidden behind the garish paintings on velvet and pulled them into the light where they could be seen. She stood back and looked at them one by one. They were magnificent. Restless. Energetic. Powerful. Easily the best she'd seen. Right up there with Jackson Pollock for God's sake.

Kristen had taken art classes at OSU. She had developed quite an appreciation for abstract and impressionist art, but she had switched her major to journalism to be more practical. She had always wondered where she might have ended up had she followed her original artistic bent.

"Have you had any training, any art lessons, Joe?"

"Naw, I'm self-taught. I got some art books, and Mama gave me a few pointers, and I just took it from there. It ain't nothin'."

"Don't sell yourself short," said Kristen. "In the right venue, you just might get a lot of money for these."

"You're messin' with me," said Joe, wanting to believe. "You think more than Elvis on velvet? Shucks, I get fifty bucks for those."

Kristen stood admiring the paintings, suddenly aware of the nearness of Joe, the twenty-something talented artist with rugged good looks. A wave of warmth swept over her, and she found herself blushing.

"I think I need to get some air," she said. "I'll talk to you later, okay? We can talk more about…art."

She quickly ducked out the door and into the unrelenting sunshine. She headed back to her concrete teepee. In the distance she could hear a crowing rooster and lambs bleating in the Alligator Outpost's tiny petting zoo. A loudspeaker cut through the air, and she recognized the voice of Billy Strongbow as he narrated his alligator wrestling show. Curiosity got the better of her, and she made her way over to the alligator pit where a dozen tourists were seated in the hot sun on wooden bleachers meant to hold many more. She sat down next to a family from North Carolina wearing soiled Wright Brothers T-shirts.

"The Indian and the alligator live in harmony, "said Billy. "We eat the alligator meat; we use the hide for shoes, belts, handbags, and other things. And by the way, you can buy a little stuffed gator in our gift shop for only $19.95."

"So, what does the gator get from the Indian?" asked a heavyset man busy shoveling handfuls of popcorn into his mouth.

"Well, we give the gators respect. We maintain the environment, so the animals thrive, and sometimes," he added, holding up his right hand with the missing digit, "we give the gator the finger. Now don't try this at home, folks."

Kristen looked carefully, and sure enough, there was a wrinkled brown finger looking like a chewed number two pencil hanging on a leather cord around his neck.

The crowd began to murmur as Billy Strongbow strode over to the edge of the circular enclosure containing an enormous alligator that had been lying so still it seemed to be made of cement. Unbeknownst to the crowd, the gator had wolfed down a raw chicken laced with a powerful sedative about an hour before the show. Billy grabbed the tail of the animal and pulled it backwards toward him. The gator's eyes opened slowly, and it gave a low grunt as though to say, "Not again." The chief lunged onto the animal from behind and grabbed its snout with both hands, and the old gator gave a menacing hiss.

"Gator jaws are very powerful when biting down, but not so when he opening up. That's how I can hold his mouth shut. Now watch as I carefully open the gator's jaws. Anybody want to stick their head in?"

"No way!" shouted a kid in the front row.

Billy knelt by the gator, holding its jaws open wide in a classic pose. Cell phones flashed in the bright sun as the crowd snapped pictures and took videos.

"Okay," said the chief, "I guess it's up to me." He slowly slid his head down to meet the gators teeth, then jerked back quickly. "Oh, man, he's got terrible breath!"

"Hey, that wasn't all the way in," whined the obnoxious brat next to Kristen.

"Old Indian saying," said the Chief in a solemn tone. "Never trust a gator who tries to get a head. That's our show."

The big man stepped through a side gate out of the pit as the gator lumbered slowly into the thick soup of the pool.

"Yuck," said the brat. "That water's doo-doo brown."

# CHAPTER 10

In a Newark, New Jersey, high-rise office building Mr. Hang Foo was becoming increasingly concerned. Leon Shively, the award-winning direct-response producer he had placed so much faith in was not answering his calls or texts. Calls to the video production facility back in Ohio brought no answers as to where his prototype kitchen gadget was, or when his finished commercial would be ready. He mentally kicked himself for ever letting the machine out of his sight, but Shively had said he needed to keep it to make beauty shots for further promotion. He sipped a cup of tea and gazed out the window at the skyline, trying not to assume the worst. The office telephone rang with high-tech urgency. The conversation that followed was entirely in Mandarin. The irritated voice on the phone represented the investment group behind the production, wondering why deadlines were being missed.

Hang Foo felt a bead of sweat creep down his brow. He made excuses, blamed the production crew, complained about the on-camera talent, and promised to get the production back on track. He hung up the phone and reached into a file cabinet for a bottle of whiskey, poured a shot into his cup of tea, and knocked it back.

\*\*\*

The heat drove Kristen back to the air-conditioned teepee. She slipped off her sneakers and sat on the bed, contemplating her predicament. What should she do? Forget about the car and take the next plane back to Ohio? Or wait for her new "brain" to be installed and have a leisurely drive back? Maybe have some time to reflect, to plan this new, unexpected stage of her life. All the while she was wishing to be rid of her husband, she had never focused on what that new reality would look like.

What would become of Dick's business? Kristen's gaze fell to the television set against the wall. No digital flat screen, an ancient tube set. She found the small black remote and turned it on. The set gave a feeble buzz and took a while to warm up. Kristen knew the production side of Dick's Direct Response commercial business very well. She helped write the commercials, audition the talent, scout the sets, choose wardrobes, and dozens of other details that it took to create a successful spot. The part she didn't know was how to deal with the factories in Hongkong and Taiwan where most of the products were produced.

The old TV set finally lit up, and Kristen began clicking through the channels. Sure enough, there was the Egger-Gizer, a Dick Lance production. That young hussy, Summer Springfield, was preening and smiling for all she was worth. "Cheap tramp," Kristen said aloud. She couldn't bear to watch more of that. She changed the channel again, and on came the news from a television station out of West Palm Beach. The man in uniform being interviewed looked familiar. It was Deputy Mike Russell, the officer who had been very kind to her last night. Now, he spoke stiffly to a reporter while the words "Canal Calamity! Victim still missing" appeared on a banner beneath the picture.

"We'll have another team searching the area this afternoon," said Russell, standing on the weed-lined bank in front of the dark canal. "Of course, the longer this man remains missing the less chance we're going to have of finding him alive."

In the background a bystander could be heard saying loudly, "No freakin' way."

The camera shot changed abruptly to a closeup of a large gator cruising slowly through the water. The female reporter's voice breathlessly spoke over the picture. "The presence of several large alligators in this canal not only lessens the chance of finding prominent television producer Dick Lance's body but poses a serious threat to the safety of these brave police divers." The picture changed to a full shot of the blond mini-skirted reporter trying to look as serious as possible while fighting to keep her hair from blowing in her face. "Of course, we'll bring you more details as they become available. I'm Katisha Merryweather, Action News. Back to you. "

Kristen's eyes teared up as she turned off the TV and lay back on the bed. Even though Dick Lance had been a real shit, getting eaten by a gator was a horrible way to go. Pangs of guilt coursed through her brain as she remembered how she had wished him dead last night. She began to cry out loud, in long aching sobs. She had held her emotions in for too long and now she needed to just let it all out. Her body convulsed as she dove her face into the pillow and cried until she could cry no more.

*\*\**

A sharp rap on the door of her teepee bungalow awakened Kristen from a fitful sleep.

"Who is it?" she asked. She glanced at the mirror and noticed her face was a total wreck.

"Deputy Russell, Mrs. Lance, may I come in? "

Kristen scrambled to her feet and reached for a tissue, frantically daubing at her mascara-lined face.

"Just a minute," she called out. She opened the door, and Russell, in a crisp, dark green uniform with short sleeved shirt walked in carrying a clipboard. "You always seem to catch me when I look like refried crap."

"Sorry about that. If it's any consolation, you look fine to me, but I understand these are very tough times." Russell paused a moment, looking around this small round room. "Wow, looks like the place was decorated by John Wayne." Sitting on the bed didn't seem very professional to him. He motioned toward a desk and asked to sit down.

"I go by my maiden name, Kristen Daniels. Please don't call me Mrs. Lance. And please sit. I saw you on TV a little while ago," said Kristen as she perched on the edge of the bed.

"Yeah, well that's one of the more irritating tasks of my job."

"So, I guess there's no new news? I mean, they haven't found...?"

"No. Nothing new." said the deputy.

An awkward silence followed as Kristin turned her head to look out the window as if to see Dick Lance come strolling across the parking lot trailing canal water. Russell frowned at his clipboard.

"Speaking of TV," he began, clearing his throat. "I have found that your husband was quite a successful producer."

Kristen seemed mildly surprised. "Well yes, I guess in his own way. I mean, it's not like he had a sitcom or made a major motion picture. He's no Spielberg. He made commercials. Those Direct Response 'As Seen on TV; Buy Now' kind of things. Some were pretty embarrassing."

"Some pretty profitable," said Russell, watching her closely. She had wiped away the tears and ruined makeup and was quickly brushing her hair. Her clothes were simple, yet stylish. A white polo shirt with the crest of some country club over the left breast, crisp khaki pants, and sneakers that had never seen dirt before coming to the Alligator Outpost. She had natural good looks that didn't require makeup, he noticed. "I've done a little calling around. Mr. Lance did quite well. "

"Yes, he was lucky most of the time," said Kristen, not knowing where this conversation was going. "As a rule of thumb, only one in ten Direct Response commercials work. So as my husband would say, you have to throw a lot of stuff against the wall before something sticks. I'm paraphrasing here."

"I get the picture. Anyway, your husband was quite wealthy, right?" asked Russell with his eyebrows raised.

"Wealthy?" Kristin seemed embarrassed by the notion. "That's a stretch. We didn't miss any meals, but I wouldn't call us wealthy."

"Well, I would," the deputy continued flatly, "considering he had an investment portfolio worth two-point-four million."

Kristen stared at him blankly. She screwed up her forehead as if trying to decipher a foreign language. "What? Two-point-four million? That's nuts! We have six thousand in a savings account, eight hundred of which we withdrew to take this cheap-ass vacation in a broken-down car."

Russell regarded her, emotionless. Testing her. Watching for a slip in her demeanor that would reveal her as a heartless bitch who might have disposed of her husband in order to take all the marbles. Could she really not know her husband had over two million in savings? She didn't look that naïve.

"Where did you come up with this two-point-four million?" she demanded.

Russell dropped his eyes to his clipboard. If she was lying, she was doing a great job at appearing clueless. "The investment firm of Randolph, Grayson, and Gleason back in Columbus, Ohio holds the account for your husband under the name of Direct Lance Limited. It was very easy for me to find. I assume it would've been even easier for you."

"I had no idea," she said in a half whisper. "This is incredible. Why wouldn't he have told me?"

Detective Russell regarded her without expression. It was the neutral, cold face he presented to suspects time after time to encourage them to keep talking, to explain their actions, fill in the gaps, perhaps trip themselves up.

"I recall you saying that you and your husband were having a little difficulty. He had a drinking problem. Anything else you want to tell me?"

"Officer," Kristen said, drawing herself up and leaning toward him. "Dick was always a cheapskate. In the way he ran his business, and in the way he ran our household. He always kept me on a strict budget. He'd always complain about losing money when one of his products wouldn't sell. He'd talk about having to borrow. He used unpaid interns from Ohio State in his office and production crews. Told them he would teach them the television business, which was a flat-out lie. Mostly they ran errands. Now you tell me he had two million dollars in investments. That's just insane!"

Russell softened his expression slightly. "Why do you think he would keep it from you?"

Kristen stared out the window as a new picture began to come into focus in her brain. Dick Lance had been leading a double life. She knew he could be two-faced. Pour on the charm to a new client. Tell the rubes what they wanted to hear. Promise the world. He had been doing that to her. Apparently not only about his women, but hiding his success, all the while socking away the profits. To do what? Run off with one of his TV bimbos?

"That son of a bitch," she said finally, not in an angry tone, but one of sad recognition.

"Well, that son of a bitch has now made you a wealthy woman," said Russell. "Assuming he stays dead."

Kristen stared at him." What's that supposed to mean?"

"With no body the case remains open. Unsolved. It'll just be a continuous pain in my ass. And you won't be able to collect any of his money."

"Well, I'm so sorry to ruin your damn day!" Kristen snapped. "Do you think this is some sort of Disney holiday for me?"

"I'm sorry, Mrs. Lance."

"And stop calling me that! I use my maiden name, Kristen Daniels."

Russell scribbled on his clipboard. "Sorry, Ms. Daniels, I didn't mean to be a jerk," he said contritely. He was torn between feeling sorry for this woman and considering her a cold, hard killer. "Listen, I know this has been tough, but I've been keeping the reporters away from here, just so you know. This is the kind of crap they eat up. They'd like to get to you, but I kind of figured you weren't ready for that."

Kristen looked more closely at the deputy and found a true hint of compassion.

"Thanks, "she said, "I appreciate that." He didn't seem like the cop type, with a softer face and wavy dark hair, not a crew cut. Maybe late thirties, early forties. Then she noticed a tattoo of a shark fin on his well-developed bicep. "Is that a gang symbol on your arm?"

"Hardly. I'm a Parrot Head."

"Excuse me?"

"You know. Fins to the left, fins to the right."

"Oh, Jimmy Buffett. Sorry." She smiled. "Your head looks completely normal."

"My old man was a fan. I got the tat when I was in the Coast Guard. I heard a lot of Buffett while I was in the service. All the Coasties listened to him. His music just seemed to be the right vibe for being at sea. Shame he passed away. After the Guard, getting into police work was an easy transition."

Kristen gave a relaxed smile. "Well, thank you for your service."

\*\*\*

After Russell left, Kristen was once again alone with her thoughts. She had copied the information about the investment firm of Randolph, Grayson, and Gleason and began making phone calls. Dick had no family members for her to call, but Kristen knew she had to talk with her father. He answered on the second ring.

"Kristen, is that you?"

"Yes, Dad, it's me."

"Thank God, I've been worried sick about you. I saw it on the news. It's terrible! Dick is missing. Maybe gator bait? Are you hurt? Do you need me to come down there?"

"No, I'm fine; don't be silly, but yes, I'm afraid Dick is gone.

"Well, baby girl," he said softly, "At least it wasn't you. Just that useless prick, Dick. Sorry, but you know how I feel. I could come down there and kick butt if you want. I'm perfectly capable of traveling."

"Not necessary, Dad. But thanks."

That night, Kristen enjoyed an authentic Southern meal of catfish and hush puppies served up by Mama Strongbow. The fish was fresh and tasty; the hush puppies had chunks of corn inside, and Kristen tasted collard greens for the first time in her life and enjoyed them thoroughly.

After the meal, Mama took off her apron and sat down across from Kristen.

"So, how are you, child?" she asked; her bright eyes were ringed by a spider's web of wrinkles. "Are you all right?"

Kristen reached across the table and took the wrinkled, brown hand in hers. "Well," she said, "I'm getting better, and I want you to know that I will pay for everything. You've been so kind."

"Nonsense," said Mama. "My pleasure. You stay as long as you need to."

"But I can pay! Seriously. Suddenly, money's no problem. I don't even know if I should bother to fix that old car."

"Take your time," Mama answered calmly, "There's no need to make quick, snap decisions. It's nice having some young blood around here."

Kristen smiled and gave the old woman's hand a squeeze. It made her think of her own mother. She didn't want to make hasty decisions, but she could see that staying in this sad place would drive her out of her mind.

# CHAPTER 11

Mike Russell was sitting in his West Palm Beach office just daring the phone to ring. He had been inundated with multiple newspaper, TV, and radio stations calling about the Lance case. Unbeknownst to Russell, the news had traveled like electricity through the tight-knit world of direct-response advertising. Everyone was talking about the fate of Dick Lance. The moment he looked away the phone gave another piercing ring.

"Russell," he barked into the receiver. But instead of the voice of a reporter trying to pry out the gory details of Lances' demise, he heard the slightly accented, formal English of an Asian man.

"Sir, you are the detective on the Dick Lance case?"

"Yes, that's right, how can I help you?"

"Mister Lance is missing; is that correct?"

Russell paused for a second, still thinking this might be a reporter. "Yes, that is unfortunately true. Mr. Lance's body has not been found."

"Very disturbing. Terrible. And how may I find you, sir?"

"I'm in West Palm Beach, Florida, Palm Beach County Sheriff's Office. Easy to find. And may I ask your relationship to Mr. Lance?"

"I am a business associate. Long time friend…long time. And, Mrs. Lance, she is in West Palm Beach also?"

"Not exactly—and she prefers Daniels, by the way. What might your name be, sir?"

"Daniels?" said Hang Foo, confused by the non sequitur. He had no idea who Daniels was. He mentally waved it aside. "My name is Hang Foo. I've had many business dealings with Dick Lance before he died. Many major productions. It is very important that I find Mrs. Lance. Extremely important!"

Russell picked up a pen. "Well, if you'll give me some contact info, I'll see that Ms. Daniels gets the message. She's not to be disturbed at this time," he said warily. The caller I.D. read Newark, New Jersey.

Russell wrote down the phone number for Hang Foo and

told him that he would give Kristen the information as soon as possible. After hanging up he researched the phone number he had been given and found it was registered to Fast Action Products of Hong Kong. Russell mused over that for a moment, wondering if that was where the infamous Egger-Gizer was produced.

Meanwhile, in his office in Newark, Hang Foo had already instructed his secretary to book the next available flight to West Palm Beach. He studied the set of blueprints on his desk, looking carefully at the specifications. He was a thin man with salt-and-pepper hair and a tiny black mustache. He squinted through his round glasses at the highly detailed drawings. "Son of a bitch," he muttered to himself as he regarded this, the most important Direct Response creation he had ever developed. This was the *piece de resistance*, the culmination of decades of toiling to make successful kitchen products out of incredibly cheap plastic. This was the Mega Meal A Gizer. Not only could this space-age machine chop, slice, dice, whip, grate, and serrate, with additional attachments (sold separately) the whole thing could be put in a microwave to cook the perfect omelet, warm up stew, heat mashed potatoes, or cook an entire gourmet meal. And it was PFOA free and dishwasher safe. It also featured a knife sharpener and a bottle opener. It was the perfect kitchen gadget.

"That bastard's not going to get away with this," muttered Hang. He was talking about Dick Lance, who he suspected of stealing the prototype Mega Meal A Gizer in cahoots with that bastard Leon Shively. Hang Foo had good reason to be suspicious. A few years before, just as his company's microwave egg cooker, the "Eggo Maniac" began to show signs of success, Dick Lance debuted his Egger Gizer, a nearly identical copy of the Eggo Maniac.

In the Direct Response business, this is called "knocking off" the competition, and it's not uncommon. Once a product proves to be successful, cheap imitations with similar sounding names flood the airwaves, often accompanied by "amazing" free add-ons and a flashy "But wait there's more!" Lance's Egger Gizer leaped ahead in sales and the Eggo- Maniac laid an egg. Hang Foo had vowed to never do business with the backstabbing Dick Lance again.

Hang lost an enormous amount of money in the Egger Gizer debacle, as well as the confidence of his investors, a shady syndicate of money-handlers headquartered in Hong Kong. They were known for their heavy-handed dealings with borrowers who failed to repay their loans.

In the beginning, Dick Lance had seemed so trustworthy. He had worked alongside Hang Foo, absorbing tricks of the trade, eagerly learning the Direct Response business. "How to sell the sizzle instead of the steak," he called it. But Hang also taught him the more practical side of the business. Where to find a fulfillment house to take all those 800 number calls, process the credit cards, and ship the merchandise. And most importantly, he learned the magic of the $19.95 price point. Most folks just don't feel like taking a chance on an item that costs more than twenty dollars, Hang explained. Dick Lance, being a greedy man, soon realized that splitting from Hang Foo and going off on his own was the quickest way to become obscenely wealthy. Of course, this would be made all the easier with a product already proven successful by someone else.

Hang Foo put his Mega Meal A Gizer blueprints carefully on the top shelf of a tall bookcase. He glanced at the singing bird clock on the wall as it chimed with the song of a canary. Each hour featured the song of a different bird. The clock was a constant reminder that even the most unusual products could become a huge hit in direct-response advertising with the right marketing. He picked up his briefcase, walked out of his office, and gave a curt bow to his secretary, who bowed back a little bit lower. He wondered what to pack for West Palm Beach. He had a feeling this would certainly be no pleasure trip.

Hang knew he had to get the prototype Mega Meal A Gizer back before it fell into the wrong hands—if it hadn't already. Had Dick Lance met with some other producer before his canal accident? Or was his creation still in the possession of his grieving widow? On the other hand, he didn't put it past Lance to fake his own death just to make a buck.

Hang Foo was stuck in traffic behind the wheel of his silver Toyota Avalon headed for the Newark airport when his cellphone rang. A glance at the caller ID made him cringe. It was the Hong Kong investment syndicate checking up on him. "Mr. Pang!" he said cheerfully into the cell phone. "What an honor to hear from you." A torrent of Mandarin expletives poured out of the phone. Hang Foo answered back gamely in his parents' language. The gist of the conversation was that Hang Foo was running out of time to make good on his debt with the boys from Hong Kong. When he confessed that his prototype Mega Meal A Gizer had been stolen and was very likely about to be knocked off, Mr. Pang advised him that two of his associates would meet him at the airport in West Palm and be his personal security guards. He would be under constant watch until the kitchen gadget was found. Hang Foo was in no position to object. He hung up the phone with a worried sigh and drummed his fingers on the steering wheel. "Son of a bitch," he muttered.

# CHAPTER 12

On his way back to his home in Lake Worth, Deputy Mike Russell put a phone call in to the Alligator Outpost. "What do you know about a Mr. Hang Foo?" he asked, skipping the pleasantries and going straight to the question when Kristen answered the phone in her teepee.

"Hmm, Hang Foo," she said slowly. "My husband worked with him for a few years, interesting guy; they were sort of partners for a while. A very smart man, from what I was told. Dick learned a lot from him. Then he wanted to branch out on his own."

"So, they are now competitors?"

"Well yeah. I guess you could say that. I'm pretty sure Hang Foo hates his guts. Basically, Dick screwed him over badly. Truth be known the Direct Response business is incredibly dog-eat-dog. Everyone keeps track of what everyone else is doing very closely. It's a very small world."

"Well, the gentleman seems highly anxious to talk to you."

"Oh? she said," I can't imagine why."

"I told him you were not to be disturbed, but he was pretty insistent. Very anxious. From the sound of it, I wouldn't be surprised if he pops up sometime soon."

Kristen was puzzled. "I guess that's okay, but if he wants to know about Dick's business, I don't think I'll be much help."

Kristin asked Mike Russell how much longer she would be required to stay cooped up in a tragic tourist stop in the middle of nowhere. He told her that she was free to go wherever she pleased, just as long as she stayed in touch and reachable. In other words, she was basically stuck. Russell was anxious to get some answers about this mystifying dead-end swamp case before giving up on it.

Once home, Russell slid the key into the lock of his 1950's era ranch house on South M Street in Lake Worth. He could hear his dog Rocket, the furry little mutt from the rescue shelter, whining from behind the door. He squeezed his way in so the dog wouldn't escape and pulled a cold beer from the refrigerator with the animal hot on his heels. He picked up the dog's leash, which caused it to jump around like a jackrabbit in anticipation. He opened the door a crack, and Rocket took off like a shot, headed for his favorite urinal, the front left tire of the next-door neighbors' Thunderbird. Russell hoped no one was looking out the window.

After chasing the dog down and getting the runaway back on his leash, Russell rolled back the tarp off his project car which was waiting in the carport. It was a 1968 Camaro convertible he had bought as a consolation prize for himself two weeks after his divorce. It was a work in progress. Mechanically sound but needing a few cosmetics, it was a nice project to fill his spare time and keep his mind off being alone.

With Rocket riding shotgun, he settled behind the wheel and nursed his beer, going nowhere. Jimmy Buffet's volcano song could be heard from inside the house singing, "I don't know. I don't know." He replayed the events of the last two days, trying to make sense of this frustrating canal case with the mysterious attractive widow.

***

As Mike Russell finished walking his dog, Kristen was back at the Outpost, taking a walk of her own. The small round room she was staying in felt as if it were closing in on her. She put on a pair of sneakers and slipped outside as the last rays of sunlight disappeared behind the trees. There was no activity in the courtyard of the teepee-shaped motel rooms. A family from Jacksonville was in the "Moose" teepee, and a couple from Oregon occupied the "Bear."

Beyond the lights of the courtyard, the surrounding woods turned ominously dark. There was no moon to wash out the array of stars that were beginning to appear, so Kristen decided to walk to a darker area of the Alligator Outpost to enjoy the night sky. She took a seat in the bleachers where she had earlier witnessed the alligator wrestling show. A light breeze lifted a few strands of hair around her face as she gazed up to the heavens, pondering what to do next with her life.

If what the detective said were true, she really had

nothing to worry about, at least financially. She wondered how she should live her life now that she was free of her husband. Could she live a life of leisure? Continue Dick's business? Maybe she could go back to her first love, art. Perhaps open a little gallery back in Columbus. The more she thought about that, the better it sounded. The loss of the scheming Dick Lance wasn't a loss at all. It was the gift of a new life. A return to her youthful dream.

A shooting star lit the night as it arced across the dark sky. Kristen took it as a sign. She stared up at the sky for another twenty minutes, waiting for another meteor, but none came. Kristen got up and slowly walked through the darkened compound. It seemed as though she was the only person in the world. She had reached the backside of the Alligator Outpost and was about to turn around when she noticed a flickering light coming from a small squarish building that looked like a storage shed. Faintly, music could be heard emanating from the place when the breeze blew just right.

Kristen looked over her shoulder. There was no one to watch her; she had nothing else to do. Curiosity got the better of her, and she quietly walked toward the building. She reasoned that the flickering light could mean a fire, so she was just doing her civic duty by peeking in the window.

The window in the front proved to be too high to see in, so she went around to the back. The glass of the back window was streaked with dirt and cobwebs, so it was hard to make anything out at first. The interior of the place was lit with numerous candles of various sizes, flickering off the walls in a haunting dance. The walls themselves were splattered with blobs of paint in every color of the rainbow and then some. Stacks of paintings were piled everywhere. Images of Elvis on velvet stared out into the murky light, the sneer perfect.

In the center of the room Kristen could see a large canvas mounted on a low easel, as though the painter working on it might be a midget or someone in a wheelchair. The painting on the easel was a vivid abstract.

Threads of colors intertwined in incredible complexity. The painting seemed to pulse in the twitching, flaming candlelight. Kristen was nearly unable to stifle a gasp when Joe

Glades stepped into view. The backside of his muscular nude form was facing her as he regarded the canvas in front of him. The flickering candlelight revealed a superbly toned body with what appeared to be a leather belt around his waist. As she watched in shocked silence, he thrust his body at the canvas. A new swath of color appeared. Again and again, he swayed, shimmied, and ground his hips like some stripper who had just been way over-tipped. It was like a no-hands fencing match. Periodically, Joe Glades would step out of view to renew the paint on his brush. To Kristen's relief she could now see that he did indeed have a brush attached to some sort of leather codpiece that allowed him to paint his creation without actual body contact. Joe had been inspired by an art book he found at a flea market which described an avant garde woman from Paris who created art by rolling around on the floor in the nude while covered in paint. Joe's approach provided a bit more control and was certainly less messy.

Kristen continued to watch. The scene was mesmerizing as the hypnotic light cast rugged shadows on the walls and on the sweating, tanned body of Joe Glades. Kristen felt herself trembling slightly as she shifted her footing to get a better vantage point.

A sharp crack of a small branch beneath her foot made her instantly duck down, out of sight of the window. She didn't know if Joe had heard the noise, but she certainly didn't want to wait around to be found as a peeping Tomasina. Kristen remained in a crouch and backed quietly away from the window. She scurried back to her teepee hotel room and closed the door behind her, replaying the vivid images of the naked artist painting in the most intimate of ways in her mind.

"No wonder Joe seemed to be embarrassed by his abstracts," she thought. But still, the end result was remarkable. The main thing was to hide from the art connoisseur which end was responsible.

# CHAPTER 13

Mr. Hang Foo turned his cell phone back on as the Boeing 737 turned off the active runway at Palm Beach International. The plane ride from Newark airport, sitting in the middle seat bookended by a rotund couple on their way to a Florida vacation, had been brutal. When the plane lurched to a stop at the gate, the vacationers, along with everyone else on the plane sprang to their feet in a futile effort to be first to get off. The diminutive Hang Foo was carried along by the crowd like a pebble in an avalanche, buffeted and bounced from one person to another. As he made his way through the terminal toward the exit, he noticed two young, beefy Asian men in identical black suits and dark glasses holding a sign that read simply, "FOO." Hang Foo gave the two men a polite bow. They stared back.

"Yo," said one.

"Wassup?" said the other.

With minimal conversation, Hang Foo found himself in the backseat of a dark Mercury Marquis with blacked-out windows careening out of the parking lot. Ear-splitting hip-hop music blared from the car stereo. They turned westbound onto Southern Boulevard toward Lake Okeechobee. The bodyguards had introduced themselves as Mr. Chin and Mr. Chan. Chin had insisted on doing the driving while Chan rode shotgun. Hang Foo was at a loss how to tell the two apart until he noticed that Chin was more heavy set, and Chan had a tattoo of Bruce Lee on his neck. The car had a strong odor of weed.

"So," said Hang Foo in Mandarin, "you gentlemen are going to help me retrieve my property, right?"

Chan turned around in his seat to get a look at him and scowled. "Speak English, man. I can't understand a word you're sayin'."

"Oh, sorry about that." He continued in English, "What I said was, you guys are going to help me get back the Mega Meal A Gizer."

"Shit yeah, old man. I hear you're in real deep. You better hope we find that damn thing."

"We'll find it," added Mr. Chin, also in English with a heavy New Jersey accent. "You're with Team Ninja now, and if anybody gets in our way, it's badda bing, right?"

"Badda bing?" Hang repeated, puzzled.

"Sure," said Chan, lighting up a joint and cracking the window. "Y'know, kaboom, lights out, end of story. Know what I'm sayin'? How do you say that in Chinese anyhow?"

Hang Foo was at a loss for words.

"You guys are messing with me, right?" he said.

"We don't mess around," said Chan in a menacing voice.

The marijuana smoke made Hang extremely nervous. Brought up in the tough streets of New Jersey and raised by gangs, these young men were definitely not schooled in the ancient tradition of respecting their elders.

"So," he asked cautiously, "You guys in advertising, too?"

"Hell, no," snorted Chan, picking up a fistful of potato chips from a bag between the front seats. "We're in enforcement. We make sure everybody plays by the company rules. They call us the dark ninjas. Hey, who's your favorite martial arts dude?"

Hang Foo eyed the tattoo on Chan's neck. "Well, Bruce Lee, of course."

"Hell yeah!"

Chin chimed in. "Bruce is the bomb. That's our jam."

Hang was getting a very bad feeling about his predicament. He thought to himself, "they're no Bruce Lee, more like Kung Fu Panda." He decided to change the subject. "Look, in that canal. That's one big alligator."

\*\*\*

Kristen nursed a cup of coffee and an order of whole wheat toast with marmalade jelly in the Outpost Cafe. She was staring out the window thinking of the image of Joe Glades, magnificently nude, creating his pelvic art.

"Well, I put it in," said the voice of Joe Glades from behind her. Kristen choked on her coffee and nearly sprayed it across the room.

"Joe!" she said, wiping her mouth with a napkin. "You startled me."

"Aw shucks, I'm sorry. But I just wanted to let you

know that I put in the new part on your car, and it fired right up. It's runnin' great. You're good to go."

"Oh." She struggled for words and felt herself blush. "That...um... that's wonderful. Okay, I'll be over to the garage after I finish this coffee."

"Does that mean you'll be leaving right away?"

"Well," said Kristen looking into her coffee cup, hoping she didn't seem too rattled. "I don't know. I guess I have to talk to the sheriff about that. But I still want the car so I can go into Palm Beach or something."

"Yeah, right." Joe hesitated a second. "You think maybe you could go talk to some big shot art dealer about my paintings?"

Kristen felt herself blush again. "Good idea! Have you been painting any more, uh, works?"

Joe looked down at the floor. "Well yeah, some, I dunno if it's any good."

"I'll bet it's magnificent." An awkward silence followed.

"Gotta go do an oil change," blurted Joe. "C'mon over to the garage anytime you like. Your car's parked out front."

"Hey, why don't you put some of your paintings in the back of my car. If I get a chance, I can show them around."

"You want some Elvises?" asked Joe.

"Um, sure, your two favorites, and two or three abstracts."

"Sure, I call them my Paris Projects."

Kristen returned to her bungalow and prepared to journey to West Palm Beach. She and Dick had planned to stop there before Dick's tragic dive. He had said he needed to see an associate of his in neighboring Lake Worth.

Kristen knew that Leon Shively had been a mentor to Dick as he struck out on his own in the direct-response business. Shively was held in high regard in the industry, having helped introduce the first Ginsu-type knives in the United States. Then, to that manufacturer's surprise, he was the first to knock off those knives by marketing his own: The kung fu Chef Set with the "Kamikaze Grip." Dick had seemed to be extraordinarily excited about seeing his old friend. What Kristen didn't know was that Leon Shively had been eagerly anticipating the arrival of Dick Lance with the stolen prototype of the Mega Meal A Gizer. With the prototype in his possession, Shively could reproduce the kitchen wonder through his own Asian contacts and have it ready to ship within weeks.

In fact, in the direct-response business having a product ready to ship is not of the utmost concern. The main ingredient is a highly persuasive television commercial. Sometimes, a product one sees advertised on TV doesn't even exist when the commercial is viewed, only a prototype. If the commercial sells, the orders pour in, and the call goes to the factory to make the product. Hence the all-familiar phrase "allow four to six weeks for shipping and handling." Why bother making a product until you know it's going to sell?

Kristen settled in behind the wheel of the minivan. It felt comfortably familiar yet empty without Dick sitting beside her. Equipped with a map of Florida from the gift shop, she started the engine and waved to Joe Glades as she eased out of the parking lot of the Alligator Outpost. She let out a deep breath as she accelerated down the swamp-lined road, feeling relieved and empowered to be in control of something, anything. To be able to drive anywhere she damn well pleased. To be speeding down the road gave the satisfying illusion of progress. She was determined to pay a visit to Leon Shively because that was Dick's last wish. She remembered Shively as being an odd-looking man with thick lips and frizzy hair who she had met briefly at a production studio opening. She could get it over with and check him off. Then, maybe she would do some sightseeing, a little shopping, then visit an art gallery or two to lift her mood.

# CHAPTER 14

As Kristen sped east through the humid Florida morning, the blacked-out Mercury Marquis carrying Hang Foo and his two over-developed bodyguards sped by in the opposite direction. Hang Foo and Chin and Chan were indeed from different worlds theirs nurtured by kung fu movies and fast food.

"Where the fuck are we?" complained Chan. "Lemme see that phone map."

Hang Foo handed over his device. "Should be getting pretty close, guys," he said, trying to sound helpful. Then, to his dismay, he noticed that cell phone reception had completely disappeared.

"I hope so," growled Chan, "I gotta whiz like a racehorse."

"Look there, Alligator Outpost. Last Chance Gas! That's it!" exclaimed Hang. "The TV reporters said the wife was there. It was splashed all over the news. Getting eaten by a gator is a big deal. This should be easy."

"Blood thirsty alligators, awesome," said Chan, reading the lurid road sign, "Ten miles. Ok, I'll clock it. Ten miles to go."

Of course, the miles came and went, and the Alligator Outpost was nowhere in sight, just another sign saying, "Last Chance, Gas! 3 miles."

"Somebody ain't too good with their math," grumbled Chin.

"The philosophers say, real knowledge is to know the extent of one's ignorance," offered Hang Foo to no one in particular.

Chin mumbled something that sounded like "Stuck with a fortune cookie freak."

Finally, the Mercury slowed and pulled into the sparsely populated parking lot of the Alligator Outpost. Mr. Chin backed into a parking spot next to a Ford F150 from Indiana with a SeaWorld bumper sticker and killed the engine.

"What the hell is this?" asked Chan.

"You got me," said Chin.

"Don't look at me," said Hang Foo, "This looks like a hillbilly nightmare. I think we're in a time warp. "

"Listen Pop," said Chin, turning around and pointing a threatening forefinger. "Let's just get the kitchen thing and get out of here, okay? It's in your own best interest, and ours, too. I don't want to stay in this hellhole a minute longer than I have to."

The three men got out of the Mercury and blinked in the bright sunlight. The heat of the parking lot was unbearable, and they quickly entered the Outpost Cafe. They walked past the shelves of tourist gewgaws, stuffed alligators, coconuts carved into monkey faces, postcard racks, and suntan lotion displays.

"How can I help you, gentlemen?" asked Mama Strongbow, not knowing exactly what to make of these Asian men in rumpled suits. The man in the middle looked like he could be a college professor, but the two men on either side of the older man looked like sumo wrestlers on steroids.

"Men's room?" squeaked Mr. Chan. As Mama pointed the way, he hurried off.

"How do you do?" said Hang Foo. "My associates and I are looking for a young lady, Ms. Kristen Lance."

"Yeah," interjected Chin abruptly, "Kristen Lance, where do we find her?"

Mama Strongbow looked the men up and down. "We have many guests here, I'm not sure who you mean. Our guest registry is confidential. Could I ask what this is about?

"Confidential?" roared Chin. "This is a tourist trap in the middle of the boonies!"

"Excuse my friend," said Hang Foo quietly. "Kristen Lance is the wife of an old business partner of mine. We're great friends. I'm a TV producer. Mostly commercials. High quality products you see on TV all the time. You know, like, but wait, there's more!"

"Really?" asked Mama as she weighed the possibility that these refugees from a Jackie Chan movie might actually know Kristen. "Well, I'm sorry, but she's not here right now, and I don't watch much TV. Certainly not those commercials."

"Son of a bitch!" exclaimed Chin, "Where'd she go?"

"I believe West Palm Beach to go shopping, but I'm not

sure when she'll be back. Would you like something to eat or drink?"

Chan came back from the restroom and the three men huddled in a corner. "What'll we do now?" asked Chin. "We gotta get that kitchen thing."

"What if it's in her car?" asked Chan, "or couldn't it be in her room?"

"She could be anywhere in West Palm," offered Hang Foo, "It's best to just stay here and wait for her return."

"All right, we book a room."

"Two rooms, please," countered Hang Foo.

"OK, two rooms," said Chin, poking Chan with an elbow. "It's like, what's the old man gonna do anyway, run off into the swamp?

"Right?" giggled Chan, poking him back.

The comments made Hang Foo nervous, but what could he do? He had no way to leave this place and certainly wasn't going to go without doing everything possible to find the Mega Meal A Gizer.

Mama showed them to the office and booked them into the guest teepees "Bobcat" and "Hawk." She handed them brochures on the alligator show, the petting zoo, the airboat rides, and the nature trail.

"This might be kind of fun," said Chin, "they got freakin' alligator wrestling."

"Knock it off," said Chan. "We're here to get the gadget."

"Hey, gotta kill time somehow till the broad gets back."

Chin and Chan opened the door to their concrete teepee and surveyed the interior.

"Well, it ain't the Ritz."

"No flat screen? I'll bet they don't even have HBO."

Mr. Chin removed his suit coat, exposing his shoulder holster with a Glock nine-millimeter. Chan did the same; he also had a gun. Hang Foo's eyes widened, and his mouth went dry when he saw the firepower.

"Guess I'll go next door and look at my room."

"Hey if it's any bigger than this dump, we'll swap," said Chin as he turned on the tiny TV. "I wonder if there's any wrestling on," he said, clicking through the channels.

Hang Foo opened the door to Bobcat and saw that it was identical to the room next door. He unpacked the small case he had brought and neatly put everything away in the tiny bureau. He sat down on the bed and wondered how long he would be stuck with his overbearing bodyguards. A pounding on the door turned out to be Chin about to burst out of his skin.

"Hey Hang, you gotta see this! They found a foot! Awesome!"

Hang hurried into the next-door room in time to see an Action News Now reporter on the scene by the canal excitedly describing a dismembered foot found nearby. A yellow tarp covered a lump in the background that was surrounded by a gaggle of law enforcement officers. A banner ran across the bottom of the TV screen. It read, "Canal Calamity Breaking News! Foot Found!" The blond reporter could barely contain herself as she shouted above the noise of passing traffic.

"New developments in the missing-man case here in the Everglades. A human foot has been recovered at the scene! No confirmation has been made if this is the foot of the missing and presumed dead, Dick Lance, but medical examiners will be studying these remains, and we'll have more information on this tragic case as soon as results become available."

"Okay," said Chan," we're gonna break into the broad's room and see if the kitchen thingamajig is there. Are you coming?"

"You'd better think this through," replied Hang Foo. "It's not a great idea to break into her room in broad daylight. Better to wait for the cover of darkness."

"But what if she comes back?" asked Chin.

"That's even better, stupid," said Chan. "Then we don't even have to break in, we just put a little muscle on the girl, and she tells us where it is."

Hang Foo got a sick feeling in the pit of his stomach. The kind of feeling you get when you eat some bad sushi.

"Listen, you guys are not going to get violent with Mrs. Lance. There's no need for that," he said as calmly as he could, but he could tell these jerks were real trouble, and things could easily get out of control.

"Hey, we don't want to work any harder than we have to, Pops," said Chan with a sneer, "but if we have to, we're gonna do what we gotta do. Know what I'm sayin'? So don't be a pain in the balloons. We'll hold off on breakin' into the room for now. Man, I need a drink; I wonder if they sell beer in that gift shop? I'm gonna check it out."

Hang Foo breathed a sigh of relief as the duo headed off in search of alcohol. He returned to his room and tried to calm his nerves, but the thought of the two of them getting tanked up on booze and then confronting Kristen Lance made that feeling come back to his stomach.

# CHAPTER 15

The farther East she drove, the better Kristen felt. As she passed miles of sugar cane, she breathed in the earthy aroma of farm country. She passed the occasional truck loaded with sugarcane stalks headed for the processing plants, and the minivan was buffeted as the big trailer trucks passed by. Finally arriving in the city of West Palm Beach, which Henry Flagler originally created at the turn of the 20$^{th}$ Century to house the workers at his opulent Hotel Royal Poinciana, located on the other side of the Intracoastal Waterway in the town of Palm Beach, Kristen pulled into a Publix parking lot to ponder where to go first. Should she check off Shively or do a little pampering after her ordeal? She decided to head farther east beyond the working-class neighborhoods of West Palm to the Florida Mecca for style, luxury, old money and nouveau riche, Palm Beach. Taking Quadrille over the Causeway toward the beach, she could see the flag-topped majestic towers of the historic Breakers Hotel in the distance. Suddenly she felt like Dorothy entering the Land of Oz.

As Kristen strolled through the shopping district, she kept on the alert for anyone famous who might be strolling the Avenue. Donald Trump, a Kennedy, maybe even a Kardashian. You never could tell. She spent an hour window-shopping on Worth Avenue and trying on different outfits, each with a more outrageous price tag than the one before it. Lunch alfresco at an Italian restaurant let her do some people-watching over a plate of carbonara. The parade of passersby ran the gamut: social climbing, painfully thin women in the latest fashions mixed with old-school retired couples dressed from another era, too formal to be comfortable on this warm day. Gaudy tourists in shorts were yakking in high decibels, snapping cell phone selfies, fat folds cascading over belt lines as they tried to curb the unruly kids they had in tow. The local businesspeople strode purposefully by, trying to make their way through the slalom course of slower traffic.

"Can I get you a dessert menu?" asked the twenty-something waitress clad in tuxedo pants and a crisp, white long-sleeved shirt.

"No thanks, just the check. And would you mind terribly if I borrowed your phone? I lost mine. It's a long story."

"No problem," she said, "There's a phone at the front desk of the restaurant. Feel free."

Kristen fished around in her purse for the piece of paper that held the number of Leon Shively. She didn't really want the hassle, but she simply had to cross him off her list of things to do before she returned to the Alligator Outpost. The phone rang three times before Leon picked up. His voice came through the phone in a tinny nasal tone as if he had a bad cold. "Hello?" he said weakly.

"Mr. Shively, this is Kristen Daniels, Dick Lance's wife. "Holy shit!" he yelled into the phone, suddenly energetic. It's you! Are you all right?"

"Well, yes, I'm…"

"Have you got it?"

"Have I got what?"

"The Mega Meal A Gizer. Tell me you have it!"

"I don't think so. What is it?"

Kristen heard a groan. "He didn't tell you?"

"Leon, it seems there are a hell of a lot of things my husband didn't tell me."

Shively explained that Dick had "borrowed" the prototype for the Mega Meal A Gizer and was bringing it to him so he could evaluate it. He didn't mention that he would be brazenly copying it for his own manufacture.

"His luggage," said Shively into the phone in a hoarse, agitated voice. "Check his bags. Look in the car. Check everything. It's very important!"

Kristen promised Shively she would thoroughly search through everything and, after carefully getting directions to his place, ended the call. She thanked the hostess for her hospitality and headed back out toward her car. She had only taken her own bag out of the vehicle at the Outpost, so she pulled out Dick's suitcase and started picking through the underwear, socks, T-shirts, and toiletries. Touching these personal items brought a wave of sadness. She stopped and brushed away a tear. No sign of anything that could be the Mega Meal A Gizer.

She rummaged through some other bags and boxes. Still

nothing. In the very back of the minivan she lifted up the three paintings done by Joe Glades. Nothing under them. But as she held the frames of canvas, she noticed a sign halfway down the street that read "AArtistic Auctions." She locked the car, tucked the canvases under her arm, and walked down the block. The shop didn't appear to be very sophisticated despite the upscale neighborhood which included banks, financial advisors, and trusts to assist the uber rich in managing their finances. She pushed the door open and peered in. A dimly lit room was jammed with canvases of every size and description. Every wall was completely covered in paintings. Statues of various sizes and styles were in clumps in the cornersalong with some copies of famous works, other anonymous figures, some statues of horses, deer, even dolphins and manatees, obviously meant to grace some oceanside condo decorated with questionable taste.

"Can I help you, miss?" a voice called out from behind a bookcase bursting with art books, reference materials, and folders with papers jutting out haphazardly. A short, balding man with reading glasses on top of his head came out from behind the case and looked Kristen up and down, his eyes coming to rest on the canvases clutched under her arm.

"I was wondering if you might be interested in looking at these," said Kristen." A friend of mine painted them."

"No, I don't wanna look at 'em," said the man brusquely. "You wanna put 'em up for auction? Maybe they'll sell, maybe they won't. If they sell, I take forty percent; if they don't, you take 'em out of here. Simple as that."

"Don't you want to see them, though?"

"Naw, not necessary. I can tell it's that modern crap that nobody knows nothin' about. But hey, you wanna try the auction? You never know. There's no accountin' for taste. You just might get lucky. Find a sucker who likes that stuff. Who knows?"

Kristen brought out the last canvas, a lurid painting on velvet of Elvis fist-bumping with Donald Trump. "What about this one?" The art dealer registered amazement. "Whoa, now that's somethin' different. That just might be a winner."

"And you take forty percent?"

"Take it or leave it, lady. Auction starts at seven o'clock

tonight."

Kristen thought it over. She could leave the paintings, go visit Leon Shively, and find out what was so important about this Mega Meal thing hidden in Dick's belongings. Then she could come back to the art auction to see what happened with Joe's paintings and still return to the Alligator Outpost before it got very late.

"Fine," she said, fishing in her handbag for a pen. "Here's my name and number."

She pulled out Deputy Mike Russell's card and wrote down his phone number by her name, making a mental note that she needed to get a new cell phone as soon as possible. She took one more look at the abstract painting with its loopy swirls of color on top of the stack and immediately thought of Joe Glades painting by candlelight. She thanked the auction man and quickly stepped out onto the sidewalk, heading back to her van, all the while trying to get the mental image of the nude painter's buns of steel out of her mind.

# Chapter 16

A short distance to the north of the AArtistic Art Auctions in a staid Palm Beach apartment, Mrs. Candace R. Honeycluster had just watched the Egger-Gizer commercial for the twelfth time and decided she had to have one. Candy Honeycluster, as she was known to her bridge club, was a chronic direct-response customer. Suffering from insomnia, she would binge-watch TV and be bombarded by ad after ad. She had the latest nonstick pan collection, a cutlery set that supposedly never needed sharpening, a pillow made from hemp and bamboo touted to give the best night's sleep ever, a closet organizer that gave twice the storage space, and a power nozzle for cleaning stubborn stains both inside and out, among others.

Mrs. Honeycluster had a shrewd plan. Instead of calling the toll-free number on her screen, she would go to her neighborhood CVS pharmacy and buy the product from the "As Seen On TV!" display in the store. In her mind, she would save those annoying shipping charges and get the gadget immediately. She congratulated herself on being brilliant.

Candy Honeycluster had a giant chip on her shoulder and was always looking for ways to game the system to her advantage. Her late husband, Horace T. Honeycluster, had amassed a fortune in the manufacture of asbestos brake linings that he sold to all the major auto manufacturers by way of kickbacks and back door deals. Wealthy beyond their wildest dreams, they moved from Detroit to Palm Beach to live the good life, but Horace almost immediately succumbed to mesothelioma. Candace was devastated. She was a tough old bird in her mid-seventies, but she still craved a companion. After a suitable time of mourning, Candace began dating among the well-to-do Palm Beach elite and fell hard for an unscrupulous cad who presented himself as an Austrian prince. She was quickly separated from a sizeable portion of her fortune and developed a rabid hatred for foreigners. The heel had had the audacity to vanish in her own Cadillac. Poor Candace was reduced to living in a small but luxurious apartment, bitterly trusting no one.

The always reliable singing bird clock on her living

room wall chimed with the call of a Whippoorwill. She checked her jewel encrusted Rolex wristwatch against it. Perfect as always. Setting her sights on the local CVS, Candace shouldered her purse, put on her favorite red ball cap, and headed out the door. A few blocks up the street she passed the front window of AArtistic Art Auctions. The outrageous painting of Elvis and The Donald on velvet caught her eye and stopped her in her tracks.

"My God, such realism,", she thought. The eyes of the painting followed her as she moved to view it from different angles. It was as if both Trump and Elvis were staring into her soul. She took note of the "Auction Tonight" sign and continued on her way.

***

After a number of wrong turns through the confusing one-way streets of old Lake Worth, Kristen found Leon Shively's house. Though the neighborhood was an old one with faded 1930s and 40s vintage homes, Shively's house was updated, stylish, and way out of scale to the rest of the neighborhood. The driveway was made of cement stamped to give the impression of real bricks. A fountain in the front yard spilled water from the lips of a busty mermaid emerging from a giant clamshell. Kristen was just reaching for the doorbell when the door swung open.

"Kristen!" shouted Leon Shively. He was a short, portly man with frizzy gray hair that stood out like he was being electrocuted. He threw his arms around her in a bear hug and gave her cheek a peck with his fishy lips. She was surprised and a little alarmed at his demonstration of affection, and managed to stammer, "So good to see you, Leon."

Kristen had only met the man briefly and knew very little about him other than his reputation as a Direct Response genius. She didn't know about his reputation as a weasel. He wasted no time in asking about the Mega Meal A Gizer's whereabouts.

"I truly don't know," said Kristen. "I looked through Dick's luggage, the boxes of stuff in the car. I don't know where else it could be. How big is it?"

"Very compact," he replied, "that one of its selling

points. Easy storage. Replace all your kitchen gadgets with one marvelous machine, and it's dishwasher safe!" Leon could sling a sales pitch in his sleep.

After a careful inspection, they found the mysterious gadget in a box hidden in the compartment of the car that was supposed to carry the spare tire. "Aha! There you are, my precious. I couldn't travel with it. Too dangerous. There are people who would kill for this thing. Um, but Dick came through, God rest his soul."

"No spare tire. Wouldn't you know Dick would choose business over safety," said Kristen.

"You never succeed without taking a chance," replied Leon. "Come on inside; wait till you see this."

Kristen stepped through the door and was overwhelmed by the collection of eclectic artwork, bric-a-brac, and antiques scattered throughout the living room. A small stuffed deer peered up from a corner. A framed print of Andy Warhol's Campbell's Soup can was on one wall, a Van Gogh print on another, paired with a Peter Maxx Beatles print. Dominating the room was a large, fully decorated artificial Christmas tree.

"Wow," said Kristen, I see you still have your tree up."

"I never take it down. It's too much work and it's depressing. I usually only come here in winter anyway," said Shively.

"You've got quite an art collection. I like the Andy Warhol."

"Isn't that something? The guy blows up a picture of a soup can, puts a color background on it, and sells it for elephant dollars. And they call me a shlock peddler."

"These aren't originals?"

"Oh, hell no. I bought a lot of these on a cruise ship in the Bahamas. Way cheaper, and who can tell the difference? By the way, there are actually some nice little art shops in downtown Lake Worth. This is a very diverse town. Very eclectic. All kinds of folks. Some call it Lake Weird."

They made their way down a hallway lined with black-and-white photos of Leon holding various products he had promoted. Kristen stifled a chuckle when she spotted one with Leon grinning like a maniac and holding a fistful of bacon labeled, "No Fakin' Bacon." They entered the kitchen, where Leon took the device out of its box and placed the Mega Meal A Gizer in the center of the kitchen table in all its splendor. Kristen frowned at the odd plastic contraption while Shively regarded it as if it were the Holy Grail. It looked like a cross between a can opener and a cheese grater with peculiar knobs and handles protruding from the sides.

"Magnificent!" said Leon at last. "You've got to see this thing in action!"

"So, this is the big hairy deal we had to drive clear across the country for? asked Kristen. She picked up a small sheet of paper from the cardboard box.

"Instructions?" Leon eagerly snatched the papers from her hand and unfolded them. They were entirely Chinese characters.

"Crap," he sighed, "Well, I'll just have to figure it out the old-fashioned way. I'll have this thing blueprinted and produce a new, improved prototype. I can have a spot on the air in two weeks."

Leon Shively was so excited his nose hairs were twitching. He had learned his chops in the direct-response racket as a young man on Coney Island, where he demonstrated miracle gadgets, mostly kitchen items, knife sets and "miracle" chamois that could absorb gigantic spills, on the boardwalk to wide-eyed pigeons.. His eyes gleamed as he diddled with a little lever that made two stainless steel chopping blades whirl around like tiny fans. "Surgical stainless steel," he muttered under his breath, pulling ad copy out of his butt. "Guaranteed to stay sharp for a lifetime, or your money back," he exclaimed. Then turning to Kristen with a sly grin, "Yeah right."

# CHAPTER 17

Long shadows from tall Cypress trees enveloped the wooden boardwalk that led away from the Alligator Outpost farther into the Everglades. The temperature had dropped noticeably as the sun sank lower into the swamp. There was a peaceful stillness, until pow! The Glock 9-millimeter tore a hole the size of a salad plate into the side of a tree. Chan snorted with laughter as a pair of wood storks were startled from their lofty perch in the tree, spreading their huge white wings with black tips in frightened flight.

Pow! The Glock spat again as Chan tried in vain to shoot one of the flapping storks.

"Cut it out," said Chin, munching on a piece of beef jerky. "What do you want to shoot one of them for? They're kind of cool."

"Gimme a break," sneered Chan, always the more evil of the two. He paused to take another hit on a joint. "I'll bet they taste like chicken. Hey, get a load of this."

Chan and Chin had progressed along the rickety boardwalk to an area of cypress knees known as Billy's Hall of Fame. The root systems of the Cypress trees created bumps called knees which grew in bizarre shapes that Billy had decided to identify as celebrity figures. He had actually stolen the idea from another Florida attraction, Tom Gaskins' Cypress Knee Museum up on Highway 27, a roadside legend that had closed many years ago.

Hand-painted signs told you to use your imagination and figure out who or what the Cypress knees looked like. One knee was labeled Winston Churchill, another Sherlock Holmes. Many were named for presidents and movie stars. One large knee with two prominent bumps was labeled Marilyn Monroe.

"What the hell? Looks like a bunch of damn roots to me," puzzled Chin, coughing up smoke.

"Hey Chin, guess what?" shouted Chan.

Pow! The Glock barked again as a Cypress knee was turned into wood chips. "I just shot JFK!"

\*\*\*

Deputy Sheriff Mike Russell finished feeding Rocket a pile of table scraps which the dog hoovered in seconds. He had just put a Lean Cuisine frozen dinner in the microwave for himself when the phone rang. Russell looked at the caller ID but couldn't make any sense out of it. "AArtistic" was the name showing on the ID readout. "Russell," he said into the phone in an official voice, wondering if this was a strip club.

"Kristen Daniels, please," the voice said. Mike Russell hesitated.

"Whom shall I say is calling?"

"This is the art gallery where she left her paintings. AArtistic Art Gallery. Good news. They sold like they were fuckin' Picassos or something. Unbelievable."

"Really?" Russell was incredulous. "Well, she's not here right now, I'll give her the message."

"Yeah, tell her I've got her dough, no problem. I run a clean operation. But listen, I'm serious. Tell her if she's got any more of those abstracts or Elvises, I can sell all she's got, okay?"

"Elvises? I'll tell her. Thank you." He stared at the phone, puzzled, then jotted down the number of the mystery caller. He wrote down AArtistic by the number and thought to himself, "Great. I'm being haunted by Elvis."

A call to the Alligator Outpost revealed that Kristen was not in her teepee, but Mama Strongbow mentioned there were some suspicious Asian men staying at the place, and they had inquired about Kristen. Russell tried to make some connection between the sale of paintings and a group of Asians visiting the Everglades, but nothing seemed to fit. He asked Mama to tell Kristen he wanted to speak with her as soon as she got in and hung up.

Russell sat at his small Formica dining room table with matching Margaritaville salt and pepper shakers and ate his microwave meal while watching CNN. During a commercial break a direct-response spot came on touting the amazing properties of a set of kitchen knives that were guaranteed to stay sharp for life or your money back. A wiry Asian knife thrower wearing a karate outfit threw the blades at a whirling target with a bikini clad model in the middle, shouting, "Aieeee!" with every throw. He then plucked a knife from the target and sliced a tomato into razor thin slices. Incredible!

Russell stared at the screen as a voiceover announcer insisted that he must order within the next ten minutes to get the free bonus gift: an oven mitt that could withstand the heat of a blowtorch yet was flexible enough to pick up a pin.

The TV screen filled with ordering information, including an exorbitant amount for shipping and handling and a reminder to allow six to eight weeks for delivery. Russell noticed that the P.O. Box on the address to send a check or money order to was located in New Jersey. His thoughts turned to Kristen. Asian men were asking about her. Why? What paintings did she have for sale? Was her dead husband an artist as well as a TV pitchman? Just when he was ready to close this case, Kristen Daniels seemed to be more of a mystery than ever. He would have to make one more journey out to the Alligator Outpost, but not until tomorrow. He was tired and Rocket needed his walk. The direct-response queen could wait.

# CHAPTER 18

It was much cooler but still humid as Kristen stepped out into the night air outside of Leon Shively's house. It had been a strange evening of mixed emotions. Reminiscing about Dick Lance, talking about future plans and new possibilities for the widow. Kristen had had no idea how many projects Dick had been working on. Leon assured her that her future was bright as the new sole owner of Direct Lance Limited. Nothing was mentioned about the illegal manner in which Dick procured the Mega Meal A Gizer, so Kristen thought it was just another gizmo that Dick had discovered at an inventor's convention. After a creepy hug and a promise to keep in touch, she got into the minivan and drove toward the Alligator Outpost. The night had dragged on much longer than she had planned, and it was much too late to even think about dropping by the AArtistic Auction house.

As she made her way west on Southern Blvd, she passed the South Florida Fairgrounds, the amphitheater, and finally, Lion Country Safari, way out on the edges of the swamp. But she still had many miles to go, and with every mile she became more and more convinced that she needed to get home as soon as possible. She had fulfilled Dick's wishes by delivering the mysterious gadget to Shively, and now she desperately wanted to leave. She wanted her life back. After getting a good night's sleep, she would be on the road home first thing in the morning.

\*\*\*

Inside Kristen's darkened concrete teepee, Chin and Chan had fallen asleep. They had picked the lock and rifled through all of her possessions looking for the Mega Meal A Gizer to no avail. They sat down on the bed in the darkness to surprise her when she reappeared. The whir of the air conditioner and the toll of a six pack of beer and an oversized joint the size of a cigar had been their undoing. Hang Foo was in his own room, watching a travel show on the public TV channel.

It was a little past 11 p.m. when Kristen turned the

Dodge into the parking lot of the Outpost. She got out of the car and looked at the darkened buildings with the feeble OPEN sign in the office window. Her mind flashed back to the night she had arrived on foot at this odd, forlorn place, and she shuddered. She quickly and quietly made her way to her motel teepee, unlocked the door, and snapped on the lights. The two strange men in black suits sacked out on her bed made her gasp. They stirred abruptly, then sat bolt upright.

"Freeze!" Chan stammered as he shook himself awake.

"Yeah, don't move!" Chin blurted, rubbing his eyes.

Kristen stared in shocked disbelief. She glanced around the room, and her heart sank. All her belongings were spilled out of the drawers and closet and tossed on the floor except for her bras and panties which had been closely examined by Chan earlier and then used in an impromptu puppet show that had both men laughing in pot-induced hysteria. Chan had carefully laid out the undergarments on top of the bureau before they had both settled back onto the bed and passed out. Kristen whirled and reached for the door. She threw it open and gave a thin shriek as she discovered Hang Foo standing in the doorway. She felt a hand grip her mouth from behind her as another hand wrapped around her midsection. Chan held her tightly as she struggled to no avail. Hang Foo quickly shut the door behind him.

"Please, please, Mrs. Lance," he said in a patient tone. "There is no need to fear. Remember me? I am an old friend of your husband, Dick."

Kristin's mind was reeling. Now what? She knew Hang Foo and Dick were mortal enemies, and what were these panty raid gangsters all about? Mr. Chin ripped a piece of duct tape off a roll and held it up to Kristen's mouth. She only managed a muffled squeak as Chan's hand was replaced by the tape. Roughly they bound her arms behind her back.

"Gentlemen," protested Hang Foo, "Please. Is this really necessary? She'll tell us what we need to know. Right Mrs. Lance?" Kristen struggled wild-eyed, mumbling against the tape.

"We can't have her makin' any noise, or screamin', or somethin'," said Chin. "So go on, ask her."

Hang Foo spoke softly, apologetically. "All we want is the Mega Meal A Gizer. Is it here? It is my property, after all. Your husband is a thief. He stole it. Life is really simple, but we insist on making it complicated. Don't make it complicated."

Kristen stood frozen, trying to decide if she should give up the weird little device. Why not? What did it mean to her? Her eyes flashed with fear and anger. Why should she let these creeps get it?

"Is it here?" Hang Foo asked again. She shook her head no. "Is it in your car?" She shook her head again.

"You're gettin' nowhere, old man," said Chan. "We're gonna have to do this our way. Do her, Chin." Chin poured something from a small bottle into a white handkerchief and put it to Kristen's nose. She struggled, but in seconds she was as limp as wet laundry. Hang Foo's heart sank.

"What the hell?" he shouted, "Are you guys nuts? This isn't a movie or damn comic book! You idiots are an embarrassment to Bruce Lee."

# CHAPTER 19

The next morning Mike Russell had just finished his coffee and put the mug in the sink when the captain called.

"You're not going to believe this, Russell," he said with disgust. "The damn foot's not a match."

"Not a match? Are they sure?"

"Unless Dick Lance was a middle-aged black man. The lab got the foot out of the shoe, and it was obvious. Probably belonged to one of the migrant workers in the area."

"So, we're back to square one."

"More like square zero. Keep on it, Russell. I want to see some results."

Mike hung up and thought to himself, "Great, that swamp is getting more and more crowded by the day." He told Rocket to be a good boy as he bribed him with a treat. He slipped out of the house and into his patrol car, heading straight out to the Alligator Outpost. This foot business was a major setback. A part of a body is better than no body at all. He accelerated north on I-95 toward Southern Boulevard as Kristen haunted his mind, and not just because of the mysterious phone call from AArtistic Auctions. He drummed his fingers on the steering wheel as he drove and told himself he'd be a fool to get involved with her, or to even think that Kristen would be interested in him.

Mama Strongbow had just finished cleaning up the kitchen from breakfast and was humming a happy tune as Russell entered the Outpost Cafe. The scent of bacon and eggs hung in the air. Russell asked if Kristen had been in for breakfast, and Mama told him no, she was surprised that she hadn't been in for her usual coffee and toast. "Maybe she had a big night last night," said Russell half joking. "I'll go see if she's awake. "

Russell knocked on the door of Kristen's room, but there was no reply. After a few more tries he got the master key from Mama and opened the door. The place was totally empty of any personal belongings. Nothing in the closet, nothing in the bureau, nothing in the bathroom.

"How peculiar," said Mama. "It's like she was never

here." The old woman craned her neck around the outside of the teepee. "But her car is still here. I have a sneaking suspicion that our Asian musclemen are gone."

She walked over to the door of the teepee where Chin and Chan had stayed. "Room service!" she called out, knocking loudly. She and Mike opened the doors to both rooms occupied by the Asian visitors, but of course, they were gone. "They were very anxious to speak with her," she said, looking out to the parking lot where the dark Mercury had been parked. "I don't like to pass judgement on others, but those men were some nasty characters."

Mike Russell hurried back to his car and headed for West Palm Beach headquarters. He had gotten a description of the three suspects from Mama Strongbow and was confident that unless they were making a run for it by car, certainly someone would have noticed three Chinese guys and an attractive lady checking into a local hotel. He had a license number for the Mercury supplied by Mama Strongbow from check-in, but after a quick search on the computer he found it was bogus. Further investigation brought no results from any hotel or motel in a one-hundred-mile radius.

# CHAPTER 20

Kristen awoke with a pounding headache. She glanced around the darkened room and discovered she was in what appeared to be a drab, windowless efficiency apartment that smelled vaguely of shrimp-fried rice. The small room contained the single bed she was lying on, a sofa pointing at a small television, a sink, tiny fridge and microwave, and a door opening to a cramped bathroom. She was lying on her side, her hands still bound behind her back and her mouth taped shut. Kristen struggled to a sitting position. She walked over to the door and turned around to reach it with her hands behind her back. Of course, it was locked. She thumped against it a couple of times with her shoulder but knew immediately it would do no good. She pulled out the kitchen drawers near the sink, but there were no utensils, no knives, no forks, nothing she might use to cut through the tape.

She then remembered a technique her father had told her about the great escape artist Houdini using when he had his hands tied behind his back. By lying on the bed, she was able to slowly work her tied hands under her butt, then tuck her legs in tightly to her chest so she could work her hands around her feet and out in front of her. She was grateful she'd kept up with those yoga classes. From there it was a simple matter of rubbing the duct tape against a sharp corner of the stained Formica countertop to rip it open and free her hands. She braced herself for the pain of pulling the sticky tape off her mouth and ripped it with one quick jerk. Free of her bonds, she again tried the door, but it was securely locked from the outside. "Hey," she called out, "anybody out there?" She pounded on the door. No response.

She explored the corroded mini fridge. It held two bottles of water and a white pint container of fried rice with a plastic spoon. At least she wouldn't starve. She pulled out a bottle of water and plopped down on the couch, turned on the TV, and tried the fried rice, which was actually pretty good. It appeared to be freshly made.

After about five minutes of a soap opera, the screen cut to "breaking news." Kristen was startled to see her own picture on the screen. A photo that had been taken the day after the accident. Of course, she looked pathetic. She was described as a missing woman and possible abduction victim. Then police sketches of the three alleged Asian abductors were shown. The likenesses were pretty accurate. The men were described as armed and dangerous, and an anonymous tip line was displayed for alert citizens to call. "At least they'll be looking for me," she thought to herself.

\*\*\*

At the Alligator Outpost, Billy Strongbow was incensed. "We gotta get those bastards!" he growled in a very un-Native American-like accent. "Sons of bitches. It's like the old days when someone tries to muscle in on your territory; you gotta kneecap em right away. Show em who's boss!"

"You're not in the mob anymore, Bill," said Mamma. "Don't get your blood pressure up."

"I need to make some calls to the boys."

"Let the police handle it. Please, we don't need any more trouble." Mamma Strongbow put her arms around Billy and gave him a hug.

"Okay," he said, exhaling in frustration. "But if they can't catch these creeps, we do it my way. "

Chief Billy Strongbow's real name was William Balducci, or "Billy Big Balls" as he was known to his mob associates around the New Jersey docks. His nickname came not only from his last name but also from his penchant for taking risks. Billy Big Balls had distinguished himself by once hijacking an entire truckload of machine guns and ammunition from the National Guard.

Most jobs were less colorful, running protection rackets, prostitution, gambling, generally doing the bidding of the mob bosses. With success came complacency, and one night after way too much malt liquor to be driving a getaway car, Billy drove into the side of a squad car with a bag of money in the backseat. After some delicate negotiations with the district attorney and the naming of many top bosses, Billy had his sentence reduced.

After a short time in the pen, he entered the witness protection program. Billy Balducci always had a fondness for warm weather, so he requested Florida, hoping to get Miami or Fort Lauderdale, maybe even Orlando. Those locations were judged too risky by the parole board, and they came up with Belle Glade, a sleepy farming town just south of Lake Okeechobee. Without any choice in the matter, the former mobster became a quiet "retired businessman." He tried his hand at fishing, one of the only pastimes in Belle Glade besides farming, drinking, and going to a rodeo or tractor pull, but that was too boring.

One night at the local Elks Lodge where he had been invited by a neighbor, Billy Balducci was introduced to a petite Native American woman with twinkling eyes and a warm smile. Before long, they were inseparable. With Billy's swarthy complexion, it was easy for him to assume the role of faux Indian chief at the Alligator Outpost, a struggling family business owned by Ella Strongbow's family for many years. As time passed, Billy Big Balls became Chief Billy Strongbow, the perfect alias to avoid any contact with his old underworld cohorts. He became an alligator wrestler, airboat driver, and huckster extraordinaire.

# CHAPTER 21

The two kidnappers had confidently left their trussed-up victim alone in the small hotel room while they went on a mission to score. "You'd better let me drive," said Chin as he watched Chan take another hit from a tiny crack pipe and swerve across the centerline.

"Yeah, that's cool brother," wheezed Chan as he pulled the Mercury to the curb. The two traded places and continued down the road into a sad, run-down neighborhood known locally as The Raw in Riviera Beach. This area had seen none of the improvements of West Palm, where shabby old businesses had been turned into hip new boutiques, and downtown condo developments had blossomed to accommodate Hummer-driving overachievers. These few blocks of Riviera Beach remained mostly poor, neglected, and riddled with crime. For this forlorn neighborhood the "trickle down finances" theory was not even a drip. For ten dollars, Chan had bought a light tan chunk of crack from a skinny kid on a bicycle wearing a gold chain over a Miami Heat jersey with a baseball cap sitting sideways on his shaved head. A boom box zip-tied to the handlebars blared hip hop. The transaction took all of twenty seconds while they waited at a red light. By the time the light turned green the kid was long gone.

"You know what?" mused Chan after they had traded places so Chin could drive. "We should give that Lance bitch some crack, that'd make her talk." He burst into a high-pitched giggle that caused spittle to roll down his chin.

"That might work," Chin replied, "but I don't think the old man will go for it."

"Forget him," said Chan.

***

Mr. Hang Foo was in the same situation as Kristen. He wasn't tied up, but he was locked in a small efficiency in the same run-down hotel just down the hall with no phone, no key, and a pint of fried rice. He tried meditation for a while but found it difficult to concentrate under the depressing circumstances. He was certain the two goons wouldn't try to hurt him, but he was totally helpless, so he resigned himself to waiting. He switched on the small TV and found a nonstop movie marathon. The annoying commercial breaks were incessant. He saw two of his own direct-response products, a closet organizer called Shoe Magic and a portable outdoor grill named The Instant Chuckwagon. Both products were selling well, and Hang Foo managed a half-smile. His mind flashed back to the first direct-response product he ever saw, the amazing Pocket Fisherman, produced by the legendary Ron Popeil. His father had carefully saved up what to him was a large amount of money to buy one, and they had spent many enjoyable hours together with it, whether they caught fish or not. Hang gave a sigh at the memory. The movie resumed with raging World War II footage for five more minutes, then another commercial break began with a cockney-accented Brit shouting from the screen. The volume seemed to be twice that of World War Two.

"Are flying insects ruining your picnic? Fight back, with the Backyard Bazooka!"

Hang Foo scowled. "That bastard."

It was a knockoff of an insect product for which he had previously produced a very expensive two-minute commercial. The spot had begun to show good results, but then the Backyard Bazooka appeared and blew it out of the water.

"The secret is the powerful insect-attracting chemical formula in the death chamber that makes bugs go happily to their demise, guaranteed!" crowed the irritating Brit pitchman. The screen showed cartoon insects keeling over on their backs with legs twitching. The British announcer was Trevor Champagne, a dashingly handsome on-camera talent who was very popular in the direct-response industry. Producers felt that having a British accent would lend a touch of class to an otherwise crappy product, even an insect trap, and for the most part, they were right. Trevor Champagne enjoyed a solid reputation as a TV pitchman who could really charm the masses. That is, until he got caught up in an underage cheerleader sex scandal. Trevor was unemployable for a couple of years after that, but he made his comeback with the Backyard Bazooka, which had become a solid hit.

"Miserable son of a bitch!" muttered Hang Foo. "So

many rats in this business."

*** 

    While Hang Foo was accepting his fate with stoicism, Kristen continued to look for escape. An attic access panel in the ceiling above the tiny kitchen sink caught her eye.

    "It's a dumb fox that don't have two holes to its burrow," she said out loud, that old maxim her father had repeated time and again during her upbringing. By standing on the Formica countertop, she was able to push the panel up and, perched on tiptoes, peered into the attic. It was impossible to see anything more than a few feet in, but Kristen could make out the grid of the roof trusses. By taking a lamp from the nightstand and bringing it as close as possible to the attic access hole she could see well enough to begin her escape. Kristen wished her yoga class could see her now as she pulled herself up into the rafters.

    The attic was musty and dank. She inched her way along the roof trusses, careful not to step onto the plaster ceiling which would have sent her plunging into who knows where. She told herself over and over not to panic. Gradually her eyes adjusted to the darkness as she slowly made her way. With twenty minutes worth of tedious, sweaty crawling, she came to the end of the attic space and discovered another access panel in the ceiling beneath her.

    She listened carefully but heard nothing, so she gingerly lifted the edge of the wooden panel. Light streamed into the attic, and she discovered this area was used as storage. She was surrounded by boxes and bags with Chinese characters. Warm air drifted up through the access door with a pungent aroma of Chinese food. She peered down into the opening and could see a storeroom below her.

    She put her legs through the opening and let herself drop onto a large cardboard box. Faint traditional Asian music came from the open door to the storeroom accompanied by a louder clatter of kitchen utensils. Kristen looked up at the attic access and quickly pulled the wooden panel into place. Dusting herself off, she looked tentatively out the door. It opened onto to a hallway. The cacophony of a noisy kitchen was to the right. To Kristen's relief, there were restrooms to the left. She quickly stepped into the lady's room, saw an open stall, and locked herself in.

"Hey, you holding?" asked a gravelly female voice from the adjacent stall.

"Excuse me?" said Kristen, her heart pounding.

"Got any crack? Any blow? I could use a little boost."

"Sorry," said Kristen, trying to be casual, "can't help you there."

"Damn. Any spare change?"

"I don't have my purse," said Kristen, "I...I've been kidnapped."

"Jeez, you don't have to give me a line of horseshit. What d'ya think, I'm desperate?"

"It's true," said Kristen, pleading to the lavatory wall. "I was kidnapped by these Chinese guys, and they drugged me and locked me in a room, and I escaped and here I am in this... Where am I, anyway?"

"You're in the toilet, honey. At Lee Ho Szechuan Palace. Some of us just call it the Ho. Not the place to be if you're runnin' away from Chinese guys. You wanna get out of here?"

Kristen opened the door to the stall and discovered a skinny, leathery faced woman with the lines and wrinkles that come from years of pain and addiction. She had matted, dirty brown hair. A torn Rolling Stones T-shirt with the tongue logo on it peeked out from beneath a filthy Miami Dolphins jacket. Her jeans were faded and soiled, and her grimy running shoes looked like they had come out of a dumpster because they had.

"Well, look at you, sweetie," she crackled in her wheezy, tortured voice. "Don't look like you've been turnin' any tricks lately."

"No, I'm married," was all Kristen could think to say.

"Like that's an excuse," answered the lady between a few hacking coughs. "You wanna get outta here? I'll get you outta here. Come on. Just stay close. Here, a disguise. Take it."

Kristen put on the way-too-big, dirty Dolphins jacket and the odd couple exited the lady's room and walked down the hall past the open kitchen door with orders being shouted out in Mandarin above the racket of sizzling fryers and the clang of pots and pans. The restaurant itself was dimly lit, and no one paid the least bit of attention to the homeless-looking woman being followed by the decidedly more-coifed Kristen in the grimy Dolphins jacket. They pushed open the door of Lee Ho Szechuan Palace and stepped out into the humid night air.

"They call me Wheezy," coughed the homeless woman.

"Kristen. Thanks for your help." Kristen felt a wave of relief roll over her as they rapidly walked away from the place. The restaurant was attached to a row of efficiency apartments that had been her former prison. She watched nervously for Mr. Chin and Mr. Chan, dreading that they might pop out as they passed by the building. They were about to cross the street when a dark sedan pulled to a stop. Kristen felt panic rise in her throat.

"Hey, how much?" A chubby man with glasses and a bad combover called from the car window. "For what?" snapped Wheezy. "Five for a hand job. Ten for a blow. Twenty for a bang."

"Not you," said the man, "Your friend. How 'bout it, baby?"

"I'm off duty," Kristen said nervously.

"Gimme a break," the guy snorted. "Get in the car."

# CHAPTER 22

In the early morning, the clanging of trash cans and the beep beep of a garbage truck backing up woke Kristen from a fitful sleep. She found herself on a dingy sofa in the filthy crash pad that Wheezy had led her to the night before. Wheezy had serviced the gentleman in the dark sedan while Kristen waited nervously on the sidewalk, her eyes darting up and down the street watching for any signs of her captors. The satisfied john then drove them both to the crumbling apartment building where Wheezy rented the sofa for $25 a week. Kristen sat up and took in her surroundings. The smell of stale beer, cigarettes, and mold made her nauseous. Wheezy had left her there and gone out again to ply her trade. On a good night she made forty or fifty dollars, she'd told Kristen. At least half of that she would spend on crack. She had made much more when she first started turning tricks, but as her looks deteriorated, so did her profits.

Kristen searched the chaotic room for a phone, but there was none. She knew she had to get in touch with Mike Russell immediately but had no idea where she was. If she could find a payphone, she could dial 911 without needing a quarter. She was just about to bolt from the place when Wheezy came in through the door.

"Hey sweetie," she slurred, obviously high. "I got you a Happy Meal." She gave Kristen the sack of fast food and plopped down on the stained sofa. "What a night. I'm beat. Made some good bucks though. Hah, had one guy who couldn't get it up, but he paid me anyway. Like a freebie. And that last guy had a real button dick. Microscopic. I felt sorry for him. You really ought to think about hookin'."

"I guess I'll consider that as a backup plan. Thanks for the breakfast. Is there a phone around here?"

"In this dump? No way, not in this place. Phones tend to get thrown through windows, and nobody pays the bills anyway, and the company cuts 'em off. No phones here."

Wheezy's speech was getting more labored; her eyes were closed as she sprawled on the sofa.

"Is there a payphone nearby?" asked Kristen. The only

sound to come out of Wheezy was a throaty snore as she slipped into a deep, drug-induced slumber. Kristen laid the dirty Miami Dolphins jacket over her and looked around the cheerless room once again as she devoured her Happy Meal. There wasn't even a pen and paper to leave a note. Kristen felt guilty leaving this woman who had shown her kindness, but the thought of staying in that hovel one minute longer made her skin crawl. She quietly slipped out the door and tried to imprint a mental image of the exterior of the place so she could find it again and help the poor woman who was living on crack and passenger seat sex. The number on the door read seven thirty-one and a half. She fixed that number in her mind and walked to the corner where a slanting metal street sign covered in graffiti told her she was on Beauregard. She repeated the street name out loud numerous times as she walked briskly in the direction of a major intersection. "There's got to be a payphone," she said to herself as she headed what she hoped was east. "They used to be on every corner."

\*\*\*

When Chin and Chan returned to the apartment where Kristen was being held and discovered her escape, they became frozen in crack-addled disbelief. They looked slowly around the shitty little apartment. Nothing. Finally, the idea that she had escaped through the gaping hole in the ceiling pierced their foggy brains. "Son of a bitch!" said Chin, "She went through the roof. That broad's pretty fuckin' smart."

"The fuck we do now?" growled Chan as he hoisted a quart bottle of Colt 45. "We don't got the girl, we don't got the whatchamacallit, we don't got shit."

"We better check on the old man."

Mr. Hang Foo was sitting calmly watching a John Wayne movie about war in the Pacific when Chin and Chan burst in. "You seen the girl?" asked Chan.

"How in the world would I have seen Mrs. Lance? You've got me stuck here like some kind of prisoner! I swear you guys are going to pay for this. Don't tell me you lost her?"

"She went trew da roof," mumbled Chan, draining the

last of the Colt 45. "Now we gotta go find her before she gets to the cops."

"How do you propose to do that? You guys are wanted criminals! I saw it on the evening news. Woman missing. Suspects are Asian men in a dark blue sedan. You might as well paint a target on your ass. You idiots really screwed this up."

"Shut up, old man, I'm trying to think," muttered Chan.

Chin sounded nervous. "He's right; they're gonna be lookin' hard for us. We gotta get the hell outta here."

"Don't panic," said Chan. "They think we all look alike, know what I'm sayin'? Besides, Uncle Lee will give us cover. I told you this restaurant was the perfect hiding place. We just need to steal a car and ditch the Mercury."

"Then what? What if she leads the cops here?"

"We won't be here. We know she's got to go out to that Alligator Outpost dump sooner or later. When she does, we'll be waiting."

"We can't show our faces there; are you nuts?"

"We'll get disguises. We'll hide in the woods like undercover ninjas."

Hang Foo gave a weary sigh.

# CHAPTER 23

The 911 operator answered the phone by asking, "What's your emergency?"

"This is Kristen Daniels...uh, Lance, I've been kidnapped."

"Kidnapped? Do you need an ambulance?

"No, I'm alright," said Kristen as she nervously looked over her shoulder in the claustrophobic phone booth. "I need to contact the Palm Beach Sheriff's Office."

"Are you sure you don't need an ambulance? I could get you one real quick." The 911 operator sounded a little disappointed.

"No, I need to contact Deputy Mike Russell."

"Are you sure this is an emergency?"

"Yes, damn it, it's an emergency!"

Kristen huddled in the humid phone booth, keeping her back to the parking lot of the BP gas station where the booth was located between the 75-cent vacuum machine and the air and water dispenser. She pretended to be talking on the phone as a carload of young men pulled up with a mega stereo thump-thumping as they filled their tires with air. The unmarked squad car of Deputy Mike Russell squealed to a stop in front of the phone booth. Kristen bolted for the passenger door and threw herself into the car, slamming the door behind her.

"Nice to see you again," Russell said calmly.

"Get me out of here, now!" hissed Kristen as she gripped his forearm with both hands. He didn't tell her to let go.

As they drove, Kristen related the story of the kidnapping, her escape through the ceiling, and the crack whore with the heart of gold. Russell let out a low whistle. "You've really had a time of it. I think maybe instead of headquarters we should go to my place—if you don't mind. Get a change of clothes, maybe you could get some rest."

"That sounds pretty good right now," said Kristen as she took some deep breaths and tried to calm herself. "What about the kidnappers?

"I think they're going to be looking all over for you, but they sure aren't going to be looking at my place. After you get some rest, we can go downtown and look at some mug shots and see if you can ID these bastards." He shot her a quick glance. "And uh, listen, don't worry, I'll sleep on the couch."

They pulled into the driveway of Russell's modest Lake Worth home. It occurred to Kristen that this neighborhood was not that far from Leon Shively's house where she had delivered the precious kitchen device. Rocket the mutt, tail wagging a mile a minute, immediately stuck his snout into Kristen's crotch as she walked in the front door.

"Sorry, standard police procedure," said Mike. "Checking for concealed weapons."

"Charming," said Kristen, brushing off the dog and glancing around the tidy living room. Mid-century modern furniture, neat as a pin. Leaning against a wall near the couch was an acoustic guitar. On the back of a closet door hung a Jimmy Buffet poster advertising a West Palm Auditorium appearance. "Gee, this place is very tasteful."

"Do you mean, for a cop?"

"Of course not, and listen, I want to thank you for putting me up." She touched his arm lightly, catching him by surprise. "Who's that in the portrait over there? She's pretty hot."

"My wife...my ex-wife. That's a really old picture. Guess I should have put that away long ago." There was an awkward silence. Russell had momentarily lost any semblance of cognitive thinking.

"So, clothing!" said Kristen finally. "I guess you still have some of her clothes, unless you..."

"I'm ashamed to say I do. Procrastination is my favorite hobby. Something else I haven't gotten around to getting rid of."

Mike took her on a tour of the small two-bedroom house and showed her the closet full of clothes from his ex-wife that he had avoided dealing with. After all, it had been over a year since she walked out on him. But it was easier to just keep the closet closed and put off thinking about the painful task of cleaning it out.

"Wow," said Kristen, "she sure left a lot of stuff behind."

"Yeah, she filled one bag with clothes, some Elvis records, and her sock puppet collection and split."

"Sock puppets? That should've been a red flag."

"In retrospect, yeah. At first, I really expected her to come right back. Days became weeks, weeks became months. Then reality sank in. Everything changes. Changes in attitudes, changes in latitudes."

"I know, Jimmy Buffet," said Kristen, smiling. "Well, she's the one who made the wrong decision. I can tell you're a good man. Now I'm going to get cleaned up."

Mike watched her disappear into the bedroom, then he took a Land Shark beer out of the refrigerator, slipped it into a Margaritaville koozie and sat in front of the TV. Two teams were playing football somewhere, but his mind was rerunning images of his ex-wife and juxtaposing them with images of Kristen.

Over a half hour went by while she took her pick of the runaway wife's outfits and enjoyed a long, heavenly shower. She looked at herself in the mirror and wished she had her makeup bag. Curious, she looked through the drawers of the bathroom and found some makeup left by the runaway ex-wife. "Thanks, bitch," she thought to herself. Feeling totally awkward, she emerged in the doorway wearing a green skirt and a red pullover top that, to her surprise, fit like a glove. "What do you think?" she asked, smiling in the doorway. Mike Russell had picked up his guitar and was noodling random notes. He stopped and took a moment to answer, taken aback by how pretty she looked.

"You look like Christmas."

He abruptly broke into a spirited version of "Rudolph the Red-nosed Reindeer," then stopped mid-way. Kristen laughed,

"You really can play."

"A bit. I learned from listening to my Dad's Beatles records. I thought it would make me a big hit with the chicks, but that didn't happen."

"I find that hard to believe. Why don't you play your favorite?"

"Okay, and believe it or not, it's not a Buffett tune." He

then launched into the Paul McCartney song, "Blackbird." He played it note for note, singing in a clear, confident voice. When he had finished, Kristen applauded.

"That was amazing, you must have played professionally!"

"Not really. I was in a band in high school, but it was just a bunch of head-banger stuff. I play now and again with a sheriff buddy of mine for the kids at the hospital. We do "Old McDonald's Farm," "The Wheels On The Bus Go Round and Round." That kind of thing. We call ourselves the Pop Cops. Get it?"

"That is so cool," said Kristen, thoroughly impressed by a man who, unlike her husband, actually thought of others.

# CHAPTER 24

A cell phone with a ringtone of "New York, New York" chimed incessantly at the back of a newsstand on a greasy street in Queens. Vito Garibaldi looked casually around to see if anyone was within earshot, threw a cigarette butt onto the street, and put the phone to his ear. "Yeah?"

"Hey, it's Billy."

"Billy who?"

"Billy Big Balls, that's who. You don't remember me?"

"Are you shittin' me? I thought you was dead."

"I'm not dead."

"How do I know it's really you?"

"Okay, remember when we were kids, and we drilled a hole in the bathroom wall at your place so we could watch your sister Sophia undress?"

"It IS you!"

"Yeah, I've been layin' low a number of years."

"Like, twenty years."

"Something like that. Anyway, I'm down in Florida, and I got a little situation down here."

"Situation like what?"

"I need a couple a guys to come down here and take care of some bad Asian dudes, no big deal. It'd be like a vacation. I'll put you up. Like old times."

"Asians? I thought you just had Cubans down there. Tell me more."

"They're kidnappers, but get this, I hear they make those crappy commercials. Like, 'but wait, there's more. Call now, and we'll double your order.'"

"Oh, hell no!"

"I was hopin' you could talk Skinny Sal into coming with you."

"And you put us up for a free Florida vacation?"

"Yeah, it'll be fun."

Kristen and Deputy Russell ran through a series of mugshots at the Sheriff's headquarters. It didn't take long before Kristen was able to identify Chin and Chan. Both had a history of burglary, auto theft, drug offenses, and bad check writing. There was no one matching the description of Mr. Hang Foo.

"I don't think he was one of them," said Kristen.

"I thought you said he was Asian?"

"Yes, but not a criminal type. More of a gentleman. Old school. I don't think he had anything to do with taking me. The two others are just thugs."

"Well, he's an accessory to the crime of kidnapping, at the very least. We'll get these mug shots of Chin and Chan spread around; put 'em on the news and see if anything pops."

"So, what's going to happen to me now?" asked Kristen. "Should I go back to the Outpost?"

"Hardly, you won't be safe there. If you don't mind, I think you should stay with me and Rocket for a while, until we nail these guys. You'll be safer, and, as a bonus, you get a whole new wardrobe. That all right with you? I mean unless you want to get a motel. I understand. There's one down the road. Not exactly five stars, but they have a free waffle breakfast." Russell pretended to study the mug shots.

Kristen paused a moment, then looked up at him and said, "If you can't trust a sheriff, who can you trust?"

On the way back into Mike's house Kristen noticed the project car covered by a tarp in the carport. Mike proudly revealed the 1968 Camaro convertible and asked Kristen to get in. They sat in the carport talking cars.

"My Dad had a 1965 Mustang," said Kristen. "He loved that car."

"I won't hold that against him. I'm a Chevy guy."

"He gave it up when he went into assisted living. That was so hard for him. Like saying goodbye to an old friend."

"I can appreciate that," he said, catching himself looking at her a bit too long. "It's great that you still have your dad around. My folks got T-boned by a drunk red-light runner years ago. Gone. Just like that."

"Oh, I'm so sorry!"

"Kind of the reason I gravitated towards law enforcement." He took a deep breath and abruptly changed the subject. "Hey, let's go for a drive."

"Really? Right now?"

"Just a quick run to the beach and back for some fresh air. Twenty minutes. We can watch the sunset."

They motored east across the tall bridge on Lake Avenue with the top down, getting admiring waves from other drivers. Mike reached into the glove box and turned on a hidden CD player. "Son of a Sailor" seemed an appropriate tune. The sun was just beginning to set as they drove through the Lake Worth Beach Casino parking area, past clusters of beachgoers and fishermen loaded down with gear who were headed for the municipal pier. The scent of salt air wafted through the car as Mike pulled to a stop facing west, setting the stage for a Lake Worth sunset.

"It's not quite Key West, but we do get some nice sunsets here," said Mike.

"Is Key West as crazy as they say?"

"Crazier. And it's so crowded now. They've got these humongous cruise ships that dock on Mallory Square and block the sunset celebration. They're like floating condo buildings. The local residents voted to not let them dock there anymore, but the fat cats prevailed. I remember the first time I went there with my family. I was a teenager. My dad found this creaky old wooden place for thirty-five bucks a night called the Randy Rooster. There was this old guy manning the front desk, dressed like a total slob, who had the most bloodshot eyes I had ever seen. The first thing he asked while we were checking in was, "You don't mind loud music, do you?" Man, that was an eye-opener. We went snorkeling, saw the beautiful sunsets with all the street performers, jugglers, wire walkers. I've tried to go back recently but it's just not like it was. The Randy Rooster is now all modernized and sanitized and goes for three hundred a night."

"Hey," said Kristen, "I'm from *Ohio*; this is like Fiji to me." The sun took its final bow and made the waters of Lake Worth shimmer with golden highlights as cormorants held their wings out to dry, perched on pilings like feathery scarecrows.

Back home, Mike apologized for not being a gourmet cook. They dined on a tough as plywood frozen steak, baked potato, and some canned green beans that tasted like cardboard.

"This is the best meal I've had in days," she said.

"If you're here tomorrow night I'll make you my Jimmy Buffet Surprise shrimp dish."

The conversation was casual and easy as they got to know each other better. Kristen revealed she'd helped design her high school yearbook. Mike confessed he was lousy at sports but was a member of the chess club. Two mismatched candles from his household hurricane supplies lent a shadowy element of romance and a red cabernet turned the surroundings into a soft blur. Kristen was relieved when Mike awkwardly offered to sleep on the couch as promised, but later, as she lay in bed wearing his ex-wife's nightie, she found herself wondering what she might be missing.

Mike tried to get comfortable on the couch with Rocket curled up on the floor beside him. He couldn't help but notice a familiar scent. Kristen had discovered his ex-wife's perfume and had spritzed it on. Memories came rushing back, and new possibilities teased his senses.

# CHAPTER 25

The next day, Vito Garibaldi and Skinny Sal Maroni picked up their rental car at Palm Beach International and puzzled over a map. "Fuck is this?" said Skinny Sal. "This place Billy wants us to go to is out in the fuckin' swamp. We could get typhoid."

"Maybe that's why they call it the Outpost, ya' moron. I'll put it in my phone."

"I was hopin' we could stay onna beach, get some sun, some broads."

"Maybe after we finish the job. Relax; this shouldn't take long. What's a couple a China guys know?"

"Maybe kung fu?"

"Kung schmoo. I bet cement overshoes work just as well in the swamp as they do in the Hudson River."

Vito chunked the black rental Cadillac Escalade into gear and swerved out of the parking lot, headed west to the Alligator Outpost. They stopped twice on the way. Once to ask directions and buy a twelve-pack of Bud at a roadside bait shop that smelled of shrimp and cut-up mullet, once again to take potshots with their pistols at an alligator they saw in the canal that paralleled the highway. They missed, and the gator slithered beneath the dark brown water. Farther down the highway, cell phone service completely disappeared, but the litany of signs began advertising Billy Strongbow's Alligator Outpost, "Last Chance, Gas!" Vito and Skinny Sal pulled into the parking lot of the Outpost and parked the Caddy under the only shade tree, never noticing Chin and Chan crouching in the thicket of bushes to one side of the lot.

Chan put a partly chewed chicken drumstick back into the bucket and wiped some grease from his mouth. He poked Chin. "What do we got here?"

"Well, it ain't the broad," said Chin, picking up a fried wing as he tossed a thigh bone over his shoulder.

"Looks like we got some goombas," said Chan as he watched the men get out of the Escalade. "They don't look like no tourists, know what I'm sayin?"

Vito and Sal were just approaching the front door of the

Outpost gift shop when Billy Strongbow, aka Billy Big Balls, burst out of the door in full Indian Chief get-up and gave a hair-raising war cry. The two mobsters froze in their tracks and reached into their dark Italian suits for their shoulder holsters.

"Hey!" yelled Billy, "it's me you dumb shits, it's Billy!"

"My God, it *is* you!" cried Vito. "You scared the shit out of me." The two men embraced in a bear hug. "You remember Skinny Sal?"

"Shit yeah," said Billy giving the portly mobster a hug as well. "How you been? Not quite as skinny as you used to be, huh?"

"Fuck you," said Skinny Sal with a grin. "At least I'm not in no *Last of the Mohicans* outfit."

"It's a living," Billy shrugged, as he looked around him to make sure none of the tourists could see him out of character. The mobsters were escorted into the Outpost and introduced to Joe Glades, who took their bags. Mama Strongbow immediately stopped humming and was uncharacteristically cold to the two men as Billy introduced them. She wanted no part of Billy's old mob buddies.

Outside in the bushes, lunch was finished. "You think these guys are here because of the girl?" asked Chin, burping loudly and throwing an empty beer can on top of the chicken bone pile.

"I don't know," said Chan picking at his teeth. "They sure are buddy-buddy with the Chief, know what I'm sayin'? I don't get it, and I don't like it."

"How much longer are we gonna sit in these bushes like a couple of jerks?"

"Sooner or later the girl's gotta come back here. You gotta be patient. Think like a ninja. Focus. It's all about stealth."

"Stealth, my ass. I gotta take a crap."

"Crap like a ninja."

\*\*\*

As the sun beat down and the mosquitoes began to flock around Chin and Chan like buzzards over roadkill, another car pulled into the Outpost parking lot. A woman about the same size as Kristen got out of the car with a small overnight bag. She wore khaki shorts and a white T shirt. Her back was to them, so they couldn't see her face, but Chin and Chan were literally itching to get out of the bushes. Their beer-infused brains didn't register that her hair color was totally different, and she had breasts that would make a drag queen proud.

"There she is. I say we grab her before she goes inside; that way nobody's gonna know," whispered Chan. Chin smacked a fat mosquito on his forehead. "Sounds good to me."

The two would-be ninjas hustled out of the bushes with all the stealth of two grizzly bears running after a jack rabbit. Still, the woman never heard them coming because she was too busy sobbing as she walked toward the Outpost office. Summer Springfield had been in shock ever since she heard the news about Dick Lance. She had decided the only way to get closure was to visit the very place where her beloved Dick had passed away. She was within a few yards of the office door when she felt herself being grabbed from behind. She let out a gurgling squeak and struggled as a foul-smelling handkerchief covered her mouth and nose and all went dark. Chin quickly slipped a large cloth sack completely over her head, and Chan hoisted her up over his shoulder. At that point the office door opened, and Mama Strongbow let out a shriek as she saw the men struggling with the hooded figure.

"The kidnappers!" she shouted into the office, "They're back! They've got her again! Come quickly!"

Chin and Chan hustled to the car that Summer had driven up in and stuffed her limp body into the rear seat. Chan quickly dumped the contents of her purse out on the car floor and found the keys. Vito and Skinny Sal were a little slow on the uptake as they were well into the twelve-pack of beer along with Billy. By the time they had fumbled their way out the door to the parking lot, the kidnappers had fired up the rental car and laid rubber onto the highway.

"We've got 'em now," Billy said with a belch.

"What d'ya mean, we got 'em? We ain't got dick," slurred Skinny Sal.

"There's only one road, get it? Your Caddy can catch that little piece of shit. Let's go, I'll drive."

Billy, still in his full Indian chief regalia, tried to climb behind the wheel as the mobsters piled in, but his headdress just wouldn't fit. They lost a little time as he struggled to remove it and carefully place it in the back so as not to ruffle the feathers. Gravel flew and tires squealed as the big Escalade careened onto the highway. Mama Strongbow almost called out for them to stop, but she knew it was useless. She decided to do the only sane thing. She called the Sheriff's Department.

CHAPTER 26

The phone in Mike Russell's house rang four times before his antiquated answering machine kicked in. Kristen had just joined Mike on the couch in the living room and given him a hug. The hug had turned into a cautious embrace and the start of a kiss when the jarring voice of Mike's irate boss boomed out of the machine.

"Russell!" barked the captain, "This thing never stops! They've got the Lance woman. She showed up out at the Outpost, and the Asian guys jumped her again. Unbelievable! That half-wit Indian chief is in hot pursuit. Get down here immediately! Where the hell are you, and why aren't you answering your damn cell?"

The line went dead with a click. There was a soft whirring sound as the tape rewound.

"How can they have me?" puzzled Kristen as she drew back from the embrace. The night spent alone in the bedroom had given Kristen the trust factor she needed to approach her lonely protector. Mike needed little encouragement.

"No one's gonna hurt you, I promise," he said, giving her a quick squeeze. In his mind he was thinking, "What timing." He didn't want the moment to end, but he knew that something disastrous was happening. Now, someone else's life was in danger, and there was no telling what the desperate kidnappers might do when they found they had abducted the wrong woman. Rocket jumped up between them begging for attention, further sabotaging the moment.

"Just when I was looking forward to a game of Good Cop, Bad Cop," sighed Kristen.

"Hold that thought."

Mike wanted to savor the feeling of this intimacy, but there was no time. They looked into each other's eyes and reluctantly headed for the door. On the way out, the phone rang again. Russell quickly picked it up. "Yeah?"

"Kristen Daniels there?"

"Who is this?"

"The art gallery guy, remember? AArtistic Art Auctions. I sold the lady's paintings. Is she there?"

Russell hesitated, wondering if this guy was legitimate. "It's for you," he finally said, handing the phone to Kristin and leaning in closely to listen in. He motioned Kristen to speak.

"This is Kristen Daniels."

"Finally," the voice said. "I've been going nuts wanting to talk to you. It's AArtistic Art Auctions calling. I got your money."

"Really? From the abstracts?"

"Absolutely, those weird paintings make women go nuts, but listen to this, you won't believe it. Two middle-aged ladies got into a bidding war over the Elvis meets Trump. They got all hot and bothered."

"Over Elvis meets Trump?"

"Yeah. Thought it was gonna be a fistfight. I called this number to tell ya, but that guy who answered never called back. What's his deal?"

"Oh, he's just a friend," said Kristen as she winked at Mike. "How much did they go for?"

"Seventy-five hundred bucks! Some old lady in a red ball cap got all worked into a frenzy. She calls next day, really pushy, and wants to meet the artist. I think she wants a private session if you know what I mean. Any ideas?"

Kristen said she did know the artist, but he was hard to reach. She would relay the good news and be by to pick up the money soon.

"Kristen," said Mike warily, "please tell me you're not that into Elvis."

\*\*\*

The speedometer of the little rental car hovered near 90 mph as Chin held the accelerator solidly on the floor. "This is all she's got; we're flat out."

"Piece of shit," mumbled Chan, snorting a small spoon of cocaine from a little plastic vial. "Have some," he said, offering the little spoon to Chin's nose as he drove. "We might need to fight these assholes. But we can take 'em. We're ninjas, right?"

"Shit yeah," snorted Chin, putting a finger beside his

nose and inhaling deeply through one nostril. "And that means stealth, right? Remember? A ninja uses stealth; we're not gonna outrun 'em in this shit box." He eyed the rearview mirror. "I think I see 'em way back there. "

"Where we gonna go? There's nothin' for miles."

Chin smacked the steering wheel. "That shitty little bait shack! Remember? Where we got the beer! We'll pull in there and hide and let 'em fly by. It's gotta be comin' up soon."

The two wired ninjas congratulated themselves with two more bumps of coke as the rental car screamed at its limits down the road. Two miles behind but closing steadily was the Cadillac Escalade with the Chief behind the wheel. The Cadillac speedometer was buried at 140 mph, and the old mob friends were elated.

"We're cookin' Billy!" yelled skinny Sal.

"Hey, don't hit no deer or nothin'," said Vito, tightening his seat belt.

"No shit," said Billy. "Ain't this great? Just like the old days."

The carload of aging mobsters never noticed the Plymouth Duster driven by Joe Glades following at a respectable distance. Joe's souped-up hemi-powered Duster was capable of almost 200 mph, but he had promised Mama he would drive carefully and bring Kristen back safely. The mobsters also never noticed that the rental car they were following had turned into the bait and tackle shop using the emergency brake so as not to light up the taillights. It slid in behind the bait shop out of sight of the highway. Moments later, as Chin and Chan were casually standing in the bait shop, the big Caddy blasted by at 140 mph. "Gee," said Chan innocently, "Where are the cops when you need 'em, know what I'm sayin'?"

"Yer right about that," croaked the gray-haired shop owner with a whiskey voice. He wiped his hands on his fish-stained overalls. "What can I do for you boys?"

Chin stared into a tank of swirling water filled with live minnows and made a half-hearted attempt at being folksy. "We was thinkin' about doin' some fishin', man. Y'know, like, some bass or some trout or somethin'."

"Yeah," Chan chimed in, "maybe catch some catfish or some of those hush puppies."

The old man eyed them for a second, then gave a gravelly laugh that subsided into a coughing fit. "You guys a long way from home, are ya?"

"Okay, okay," said Chin getting impatient. "We don't know shit about fishin', but we want to try. We want to rent a boat."

"Ever run a boat before?"

"Yeah, sure, with my dad, a long time ago. I remember how," Chin lied.

"Well, you can't do much to mess up these old rigs. Long as you don't drown yerself."

The old man led them out the back door of the bait shack to a row of banged up Jon boats tied to a rickety wooden pier. The pier wobbled beneath their weight as he told them how to squeeze the bulb for the fuel line, use the choke when the engine was cold, and where the life vests were. "Kind of bait you boys want?" asked the old man with a skeptical grunt. "Worms, minnows, shiners?"

"Worms," said Chan. "Worms are good."

As the old man reentered the bait shack and reached into a bucket of dark brown earth filled with wiggling worms, the foul-smelling handkerchief of Chan came swiftly to his nose. His arms flailed briefly, and he crumpled backwards into Chan's grasp. He then laid the old guy gently on the rough wooden floor. "Sweet dreams, old man," said Chin as he laid a bamboo fishing rod across the old guy's chest. "Okay, let's load her up." The two thugs retrieved Summer Springfield's slumbering body from the rental car and stumbled down the steps to the wobbly pier and the waiting Jon boat.

"I hope this doesn't turn out to be a stupid idea," said Chin as they dumped the hooded figure into the boat. "I'm not a very strong swimmer." The air smelled like swamp water and fish guts.

"Relax, we'll be fine. Nobody's lookin' for us in a boat. We go up this canal, see? I mean it follows the road, right? We get to the end of the canal, we steal another car, and we disappear, get it? Hey, boat gangstas. Miami Vice. Crockett and

Tubbs."

"This don't look nothin' like Miami Vice," said Chin, picking up a dead minnow out of the bottom of the boat and flicking it into the tea-brown water. "Know what I'm sayin'?"

Chin went back into the bait shop for provisions while Chan positioned himself in front of the 25 horsepower Johnson outboard. He yanked the pull starter with a mighty jerk. Nothing. He did it again, and again, then remembered the choke. With the choke pulled out the Johnson started with a wheeze and a cloud of blue smoke. Chin returned to the boat with two straw hats, three six-packs, and a large box of beef jerky. With their straw-hat disguises on, they untied the boat, and Chan put the motor in gear with a clunk. The boat lurched forward, throwing Chin off balance. He wound up flat on his back on the muddy floor of the boat. As Chan gained confidence, he opened the throttle more and more until the little Johnson was flat out. The little boat struggled to get up on plane. Cars periodically whizzed past the strange trio on the road paralleling the canal. Chan popped a beer as he fumbled to keep the straw hat on his head. "Just like Crockett and Tubbs!" he shouted.

# CHAPTER 27

Joe Glades passed the bait shack with a muffled roar as he scanned the road ahead. He didn't like going this fast in an area that might produce a hapless raccoon, armadillo, opossum, or other potential roadkill with no way to stop in time. The fishing skiff with two straw-hat-wearing fishermen never would have caught his eye if it hadn't been for how low it was riding in the water and what appeared to be a large lump of dirty laundry in the bow of the boat. He let his car fly by, but he watched the boat intently. Something was off. This was no pair of local yokels.

Joe drove the Duster down the highway to a point wide enough to make a U-turn, then started back toward the bait shack at half the speed he had been doing. Within minutes he sighted the Asian duo plowing along the canal, tossing beer cans into the water.

"Not only are they kidnappers," he thought with disgust, "they're litterers."

Joe continued on to the bait shack. He slid to a stop in the dirt parking lot and ran through the open door where he immediately came upon the slumbering body of the grizzled bait shop owner, a man he had known all his life. He knelt over him and felt for a pulse. Relieved to find one, he ran out the back of the shop and down the wobbly planks to a waiting Jon boat. He was quickly underway and making twice the speed of the kidnappers in their overloaded boat. He took an abrupt right turn through an almost invisible opening in the green sawgrass. This was home for him. Few people knew this trackless waterway wilderness like he did. The blades of sawgrass scraped and whipped at the sides of the Jon boat as he sped through the shortcut. He knew he would quickly catch the kidnappers in their slower vessel. He strained to look for submerged logs and wayward alligators. Startled turtles plopped into the dark water from their driftwood perches as he raced by.

\*\*\*

The Caddy full of elderly mobsters was still running flat

out, engine straining. "I don't like it," muttered Billy as he scanned the road ahead. "This don't make sense. We should have caught 'em by now."

Up in the distance he saw a sight that would chill the hearts of any criminal mind. A roadblock. By the time Billy realized what he was headed for at 140 mph he was nearly upon the blockade of sheriffs' cars. He slammed on the brakes and slid to a stop, inches from a collision.

"What's your hurry, gentlemen?" asked the deputy in charge. He was a tall, imposing man with mirrored sunglasses and a shaved head beneath his crisp sheriff's hat.

"I know me go too fast, blurted Billy in his lame Indian chief dialect. "Sorry. We chase bad men."

"I know," said the deputy, peering into the Caddy and sizing up the occupants. "We got the call that you were in pursuit of suspected kidnappers. Sir, we can't have you taking the law into your own hands. "

"Me understand. Want to help."

"Well, I understand your concern, but you can help by turning around and going back to the Outpost. Let the authorities handle this."

While the confrontation took place at the roadblock, the hum of a Johnson outboard could barely be heard as the Asian thugs cruised the little Jon boat right past the scene. The straw hats were pulled low over their faces, and they made a point of waving their fishing poles about like divining rods as though they were about to make a mighty cast. No one paid any attention to them.

The deputy bent down to look into the Escalade and frowned, "You guys from the same tribe?"

Skinny Sal squirmed in his seat. "Na, we're from up North. Where, uh, the buffalo roam."

"Really? I'm gonna let you guys go on back to the Outpost and chill out, okay? We can handle this."

"I fuckin' doubt it," piped up Vito from the backseat. "If they ain't between the Outpost and the roadblock that means you lost 'em."

Billy whirled around in his seat. "The officer is right. We go back and let them handle this. Good luck, sir, let me know if we can be of help." Billy backed the Caddy up and turned back down the two-lane road. The deputy watched them go with some skepticism. He could swear he heard the one in the back mention something about Barney Fife.

# CHAPTER 28

The kidnappers congratulated each other on their getaway as they droned on down the weed-choked canal. In the distance a boat ramp and parking lot full of scruffy cars and boat trailers marked a public recreational area that gave the locals access to the Everglades. Chan slowed the boat and scanned the area for cops and a likely getaway car. There was no activity except for a pickup truck with trailer and boat attached backing down the ramp. A middle-aged man wearing ratty camouflage and a bent straw hat got out of the noisy, idling truck carrying a cooler, which he put in the boat. Then he began slowly unwinding the winch. The Jon boat slid smoothly off the trailer into the calm water and the man, holding onto a rope, guided the boat away from a clump of cattails. Chin and Chan smacked their boat into the dock with a crunch and were just about to tie up when they heard another approaching boat. Joe Glades was closing fast. Chin and Chan weren't sure who he was, but they knew they couldn't take any chances.

"Get the girl up!" barked Chan. "Wake her up."

Chin grabbed the woman with the bag over her head and stood her up. She sputtered to life and ripped the bag off her head.

"What the hell? Where am I? This is sucky-doo!"

Chin's jaw dropped in boozy confusion. "Who are you?"

"That's the wrong girl!" Chan yelled, as they all stood in the little boat, rocking back and forth precariously.

Joe Glades came up alongside and yelled, "Hold it right there!"

Chan gave the groggy would-be starlet a push. She screamed as she splashed into the warm brown water. Chin and Chan scrambled up onto the dock as Joe quickly jumped into the water to save the flailing woman. The camo-dressed fisherman stared dumbstruck at what was happening, even as Chin and Chan quickly circled behind him, got in his pickup truck, and pulled away, trailer and all. The water was only four feet deep, and Summer Springfield soon realized she could stand on the muddy bottom.

"Are you all right?" asked Joe, holding her tight as she squirmed frantically.

"Oh, I'm just perf! I almost drowned! I'm soaking wet! This is insane! Who are you?"

Joe let her go and stuck out his hand. "Howdy, ma'am, my name's Joe."

Summer's brain raced with thoughts of Stranger Danger taught in grade school.

"That sounds fake. I don't know any Joes."

"No, really, that's my name. Joe Glades."

"Now that really sounds fake. Do you think I'm dumb-oh? Where did you come from?

"Okay, I know this sounds weird, but I'm from the Alligator Outpost where you were kidnapped. I was chasing those guys in this boat, but when you went into the water the bad guys got away. Let me help you up onto the dock."

Summer pulled herself up a ladder and stood soaked and bewildered on the dock. "I want an Uber!" she shouted.

"Not gonna happen way out here. If you'd just get in my boat I'll take you back to your rental car; I promise." Joe caught himself staring at Summer's soaking-wet T shirt which was spectacularly transparent. He averted his eyes and pointed down the canal. "It's just a couple of miles that way. You can get your car and go back to the Outpost and get cleaned up, safe and sound."

Summer glanced around the boat launch ramp with the feeling of being watched. The camo-clad fisherman was holding the rope to his bobbing boat, staring transfixed with mouth agape at this beautiful swamp apparition, apparently unaware that his truck and trailer were long gone.

Joe had a tough time convincing Summer to get into his boat, but finally she relented when she realized the only alternative was to be stuck in the middle of nowhere with the camo-guy with a goofy grin on his face. They motored through the sawgrass at a more sedate pace than before, and Joe pointed out various wildlife along the way. Summer was not interested, and remained stone-faced during the ride, reeling from the drugging and abduction. And who was this handsome stranger? Nothing made sense. Summer's T shirt had nearly dried in the warm sun by the time they arrived at the bait shack. The old shop owner was pacing up and down the dock in an agitated rant, spouting a cloud of obscenities to no one in particular.

"Joe!" the old man shouted as he recognized Joe Glades pulling up to the dock. "You see where those sonsabitches took my boat? Motherfuckers gassed me. Knocked me out cold. I got my shotgun loaded, and I'm ready to use it!"

"I know, Harry," said Joe, tying the boat to the dock. "Your boat's up at the Loxahatchee ramp. It's safe, but the bastards got away. At least this lady here is all right. "

"They gassed me too!" blurted Summer. "I was nearly killed! I want the police. I want the FBI! I want those guys locked up where the rain don't shine!"

Joe and Harry looked at each other quizzically. She sprang to her feet in the tiny boat and promptly lost her balance, falling backwards into the drink. She coughed up water as she popped up. Joe Glades couldn't help giving a chuckle as he reached down from the wobbly dock.

"Lady, you're all wet all over again," he said, and pulled her up onto the dock with his brawny long arms.

"Well, that's a duh! Don't state the obv! Please, get me away from this drippy yuck!" she sputtered.

Old Harry eyed Summer up and down in her transparent splendor and exhaled sharply. "Well, I guess I've seen everything. Little lady, you've made an old man happy to be alive. If this was a wet T shirt contest, I'd declare you the winner." Suddenly, she realized just how completely exposed she was and chastely folded her arms across her chest.

*** 

Swamp water pooled on the floor of Summer's rental car as she followed Joe's Plymouth Duster back to the Outpost. She met Mama Strongbow and checked in to a motel teepee. She wasted no time taking a hot shower and changing into dry clothes, then lay down to try to settle her nerves. She re-ran the nightmare of her obduction and subsequent rescue in her mind and thought, "What have I gotten myself into?" She had just regained her composure when a knock at the door startled her.

"Who is it?"

"Sheriff's office, ma'am."

She opened the door to the sight of Deputy Mike Russell and Kristen. The two women locked eyes, and a shiver went up Summer's spine.

"You!" said Summer.

"You!" said Kristen. "What are you doing here?"

"I...I had to find out more about Dickie," she stammered, then began to sob. "There was so little news back home, it's so trag...so sad...Dick taught me so much about...acting, you know."

"I know," said Kristen, flatly. She gave Summer an awkward pat on the shoulder and thanked her for her concern. She had always hated Summer for her flagrant relationship with Dick, but what did it matter now? For her part, Summer suddenly felt a wave of guilt. She had always hoped that Kristen would be hit by a bus or contract some incurable disease so she could have Dick all to herself, but now she felt embarrassed, empty, and confused. Tears ran down her cheeks.

Mike Russell brushed aside this awkward reunion and began questioning Summer about her abduction and how the kidnappers managed to get away. Kristen watched in silence as she was reminded of her first visit from Mike Russell the night of Dick's death. She admired the smooth, professional, and very sympathetic way he went about his job. Mike was everything Dick Lance was not. Then an uneasy feeling came over Kristen as Summer dabbed at her eyes with a tissue while telling her tale with a quivering voice. It was jealousy. Again. What if this little tart Summer set her sights on Mike Russell? Kristen mentally kicked herself for letting her mind run away with such wild thoughts. Still, she had to admit, this would-be actress was damn cute.

After wrapping up the interview with Summer, Mike and Kristen were making their way to the parking lot when they ran into Joe Glades.

"Joe, guess what," said Kristen proudly, "We sold your paintings!"

Joe took a few seconds to process the words. "You sold 'em? Really? To who?"

"At an art auction. People loved them. We got some decent money, too."

Joe was incredulous. "More than fifty dollars?"

"Thousands, Joe, thousands! I want to get some more paintings from you so we can follow up and sell more."

"Yeah," added Mike, "I admit I didn't ever see your paintings, but I talked to the man on the phone. He was ecstatic. Looks like you're a big hit."

"Wow, I don't know what to say. People like 'em that much? I've gotta tell Mama. Wait, let me go pick out two more for you right now. I've been experimenting with some, uh, different techniques. Don't move!"

Joe ran off into the gift shop and burst back through the door in seconds carrying two more canvases. Mike picked one up and held it at arm's length. He raised his eyebrows. "Hmm, that's very, uh, quite different."

"Officer?" said Joe quietly, "It's upside down.

# CHAPTER 29

Leon Shively had completely disassembled the Mega Meal A Gizer, photographed all the parts, numbered them, and written a description, then reassembled the whole thing. He methodically fed different foods into its hopper, coming up with ad copy as he went. "It slices and dices, grates and serrates, purees, chops and shreds. Cut up chicken for chicken salad, slice onions without shedding a tear. Make coleslaw in half the time. Slice potatoes for tasty French fries. The blades are so sharp, you can even crush ice for smoothies. Even cuts through bone! And when you're finished, cleanup's a breeze!" He chuckled to himself as he fed a cucumber into the apparatus and perfect slices came flying out onto a platter.

Even though he had directed the initial spot for Hang Foo, he had already discovered many ways to improve on it for his own production. He picked up a carrot and jammed it toward the hopper, but slipped and carelessly got his index finger too close to the whirling blades. In an instant, his finger was lacerated and squirting blood onto the tabletop.

"Damn it!" he shouted, wincing in pain. He ran to the bathroom and rummaged through the medicine cabinet for a bandage. With his finger tightly wrapped and the blood cleaned up, he sat back down and made another entry in his notebook. "Caution, blades are extremely sharp. Put warning on box for liability issues." He poured himself a Scotch as a pain reliever and sat back to contemplate.

The machine was everything that he promised Dick Lance it would be. This one really did work! Housewives would rush to their phones to buy one for $19.95 plus shipping and handling. After it proved itself in the US, they would hit Europe and price it in euros. Asia would follow: Japan, Korea, Philippines, Australia. Every corner of the earth with a cable or satellite dish would be easy pickings. Finally, it would end up on retail store shelves with a little sticker that proclaimed, "As Seen on TV!" An absolute gold mine! Shiveley pondered the next step: what to rename the product. It had to be different from the competition they were knocking off, but not too different. It had to be fabulous.

He sat down with a piece of paper at the kitchen table and began a list of possibilities. The Maxi Meal Maker. The Kitchenater 2000. The Chef's Mate Plus. He spoke the names out loud to get a feel for them. He wished that Dick Lance were there to help with the creative process. Dick had a great mind for B.S. Suddenly, inspiration struck like a lightning bolt. He wrote down in all caps: THE KOMPLETE KITCHEN KING. He stared at the paper with satisfaction, rubbery lips dripping saliva. He particularly liked spelling complete with a "K". Made it special. He would immediately register the name, then send the photos, descriptions, and specifications to his source in Hong Kong.

He needed to get a note to his animator so he could illustrate the secret workings of the device so even an idiot could understand it. Shively poured himself another Scotch and celebrated his new, stolen creation. This was going to be big.

\*\*\*

Billy Strongbow, AKA Billy Big Balls, was still fuming over the escape of the kidnappers. "Stupid cops," he growled as he stared at his poker hand. Skinny Sal and Vito grunted in agreement. The small backroom at the Outpost was fogged by a cloud of cigar smoke.

"What I don't get," said Vito, "is how two Chinese dudes dressed like Bruce Lee on Halloween can just disappear in an area that's mostly white Anglos and a few Cubans and Mexicans. Where do they go to disappear?"

"Chinatown," said Skinny Sal as he laid his cards down. "I fold." "Wait, that's it!" exclaimed Billy. "Of course, Chinatown."

"Florida don't have no Chinatown," scoffed Vito.

"Yeah, but there's lots of Chinese restaurants. A lot of laundries, too."

"Not a bad idea," said Skinny Sal. "All we gotta do is check out all the Chinese businesses in the area. Go door-to-door, kinda like the old days when we ran the protection racket. Maybe twist a few arms here, bloody a few noses there."

"I can't get mixed up in doin' any real muscle work,"

sighed Billy. "That would put me in dutch with the witness protection program."

"Don't worry, me and Sal will do the heavy lifting," said Vito. "We'll start tomorrow. Get a list of Chinese joints and smoke the bastards out."

"Stupid cops," snorted Sal.

"Shouldn't be too hard," chuckled Billy as he laid a straight flush on the table and held his beer up in a salute to the new caper. "They look like the Chinese Blues Brothers."

# CHAPTER 30

Chin and Chan had scored an eight ball and were high as kites in a dingy apartment in the back of Lee Ho's Szechuan Palace. A half-eaten sack of crab rangoon lay on the coffee table, and an old episode of *Walker Texas Ranger* played on the TV. "Chuck Norris wouldn't last five minutes against Bruce Lee," said Chin with a burp. "Chuck Norris wouldn't last five minutes against my grandma, know what I'm sayin'?"

"Chuck schmuck."

"Up Chuck."

"Fuck Chuck." They laughed hysterically.

Chin and Chan were exceedingly lucky to have a room behind Lee Ho's. A shipping container full of illegal Chinese immigrants had just landed at the port of Palm Beach, and they were now all housed at the restaurant, as many as eight to a room. They had been tricked into making the long, circuitous voyage at a cost of eight to ten thousand dollars apiece with the promise of good jobs in the IT industry but discovered they would have to pay their debts by living in virtual slavery to their human smuggler bosses. The final passage of the leg from the Bahamas wasn't as bad as most, only two died in the cramped, squalid quarters of the metal shipping container. A portable fan powered by a car battery was the only means of ventilation. The bathroom was a 5-gallon bucket.

As the wretched group snuck out of their container under the cover of darkness to a waiting U-Haul, they paused and stretched, breathing the fresh air deeply, fascinated by the muted lights of Palm Beach society flickering in the distance across the Intracoastal Waterway.

\*\*\*

Joe Glades and Summer Springfield stared in disbelief at the cypress knees along the boardwalk behind the Alligator Outpost. "That one used to look like JFK, till somebody vandalized it."

"Bummer. Why would somebody do that?" asked Summer, examining the splintered wood. That's sicko."

"People stink," said Joe. "A lot of folks don't appreciate the outdoors, nature, and all that. Especially the stupid people who visit the Outpost. Most of them think it's a joke. Alligator wrestling and plastic pink flamingos, fake bird turds on a souvenir hat. Hey look!" Joe pointed towards a clump of cattails and spoke in a whisper. "See him?"

"See what?"

"A great blue heron, just over there. "

At first, she saw nothing; then, Summer recognized the bird when it moved slightly. It had to be nearly three feet tall, intently stalking the swamp water for food.

"That bird is humong!" she exclaimed, which caused the heron to squawk agitatedly and flap into the sky on long graceful wings. "Sorry. Wow, that was a ha-ha moment."

"A what?"

"You know, a ha-ha moment."

"You mean an "aha" moment."

"Whatever…"

"That's okay, I'll have to teach you to move like an Indian."

"Don't you say Native American?"

He frowned, "Nah, nobody says that out here. I'm only half Indian anyway. On my Mama's side."

Summer found herself becoming more at ease with Joe. She admired his knowledge of the vast variety of nature in the swamp and felt protected by his presence. Realizing that Joe had very likely saved her life gave her a feeling of gratitude and attraction to him. His rugged good looks didn't hurt either.

"Y'know, Joe," she said, following closely back on the boardwalk, "You are so smart. Most people can't smell the forest for the trees."

He chuckled, "Thanks, Summer, I appreciate that."

For his part, Joe Glades had never known a woman as knock-dead gorgeous as Summer Springfield. His highest level of achievement in the dating game had been taking the Clearwater Catfish Queen, Laura Lee Hicks, to a tractor pull. Laura Lee had abruptly dumped Joe for a wealthy boy whose father owned a string of pig farms. Joe was relieved because the girl made him nervous. There was no time for nervousness in the way Joe and Summer had been thrust together by fate. She was easy to talk to even though her speech patterns sometimes made little sense.

They walked slowly and silently along the rickety boardwalk, trying not to disturb the wildlife. Fading sunlight filtered through the trees as the air took on the quiet stillness of a church. Suddenly, a snarl and a hissing sound escaped from the bushes just ahead. Joe motioned Summer to be still, then slowly moved forward. After three more quiet steps he motioned Summer to join him. She wordlessly crept forward and stared into the thicket. A pair of raccoons were humping away in Everglades ecstasy, snarling, hissing and nipping, oblivious to Summer and Joe. The two looked at each other and stifled a giggle, then burst out laughing as they backed away from the amorous coons.

# CHAPTER 31

Chin and Chan were in deep slumber when Chan's cellphone rang with the theme from *Enter the Dragon*. They were out cold from a night of partying, so no amount of music could rouse them. The message they would retrieve from the phone the next day proved to be a very important one from headquarters in Hong Kong. The company that Leon Shively had sent the specifications for his supposedly all-new Komplete Kitchen King was a subsidiary of the very same manufacturer who had produced the prototype of the Mega Meal A Gizer. He had unwittingly sent his new discovery to the same people he and Dick Lance had stolen it from.

"Ain't that some shit," said Chan after listening to the full message, complete with Shively's address in Lake Worth. "Now we know who's got the machine and where he lives."

Chin and Chan popped two beers and smacked them together. They discussed strategy and decided to wait until dark so that they could move in and out of the shadows, descending on their unsuspecting target like masterful ninjas.

\*\*\*

The sun was just beginning to set as, against his better judgment, Mike Russell drove Kristen toward Leon Shively's house. He had refused at first, but she was intent on selling more paintings for Joe while Mike stayed glued to the case.

"It's only a few blocks from your place in Lake Worth. I was there once. He's an art lover." said Kristen cheerfully. "He'll drive me back to your house after the auction. Joe could use the money. And you need to catch those bastards."

"No worries, I have my junior G-man detective kit ready. They won't get away. But seriously, I don't want you out in public. I don't want to lose you again."

"I'll be fine. Leon will watch out for me. I don't think our suspects are the artsy-fartsy types who'll be going to an auction." She opened the car door, but instead of getting out, she leaned over and gave Mike a quick peck. They locked eyes and gave in to a much longer, more sensuous kiss.

"Junior G-man, huh?" said Kristen. "I think you're ready for a promotion."

"I'm looking forward to the exam."

Mike followed her to the door and was introduced to Leon Shively, who was sporting a loud striped blazer that screamed "used car salesman." Mike's immediate thought was total skepticism. Could this slimeball really be expected to keep Kristen safe? Shively stuck out his hand.

"Nice to meet you, officer. Don't worry, I'll take good care of the little lady."

"You know anything about this art place?"

"Oh, yeah. I've been there a few times. Totally safe. Mostly a bunch of wealthy old biddies. Biggest danger is getting run over by a walker."

Mike was still dubious. "And you'll drop her at my place as soon as it's over?"

Shively raised his bushy eyebrows. "Your place? Sure, I get it. Not a problem."

"Okay, then. I know she's determined to sell the paintings, but please, just be careful." He warily bid them goodnight.

*** 

Armed with the two Joe Glades canvases, Shively drove Kristen in his aging Mercedes across the causeway and up to Palm Beach. They made their way into the cramped, filled-to-capacity back room of AArtistic Art Auctions and handed the paintings to the owner, whose eyes lit up at the sight of them. Well-dressed art patrons were fanning themselves with their bidding paddles as the feeble air conditioning labored to keep up. Finding two folding chairs in the back, they quickly sat as the room erupted in noisy chatter following the bang of a gavel. A watercolor depicting flamingos standing in a pond had just sold for twelve thousand dollars.

"I wouldn't hang that up in a doghouse," said Shively in a loud whisper. The lady seated next to him hissed, "Would you please be quiet!"

The auctioneer was a tall, thin man wearing a Western

suit and cowboy boots. He looked as though he should be auctioning cattle, not works of art. Kristen observed the sweaty owner of the place, hustling the paintings up to an easel for all to see. Joe Glades had provided two more of his special abstracts to see what they would bring. The first canvas was placed on the easel and the crowd grew quiet. Then the murmuring began.

"Oh, yes." "I feel that." "Mmmmm." "Magnificent."

"Okay, now," said the auctioneer. "Here, we have a very uh, unique piece." He paused and squinted at the abstract, which looked like a tornado had swirled across a paint factory, but in the center was a very detailed portrait of Donald Trump in an Elvis jumpsuit complete with cape and outrageous sideburns.

"The artist is J. Glades. A very distinguished, uh, practitioner of the uh, abstract movement. Combining abstract and portraiture in this work. Highly creative. Very bold. Fine colors, nice balance, very powerful, don't you think?

A woman cried out from the crowd. "I want it now!"

"Who will start the bidding at five hundred?"

A paddle shot up from a middle-aged woman in the front row, but twelve other paddles shot up almost in unison around her. The auctioneer paused for a second, then said, "We have five, who will make it six? Thank you, ma'am, six now seven, six now… We have seven, who will make it eight? Let's just jump to a thousand. I've got a thousand. Who will make it fifteen hundred?"

The bidding came fast and furious as the women in the audience lunged and screamed out their bids. There was a frantic sense that someone was going to slam a folding chair over someone else's head like a championship wrestling match.

The auctioneer was speaking a mile a minute as the bids rose at a dizzying pace one after another. Two women were constantly one-upping each other, waving their paddles in the air like knights at a joust. "Fourteen? All done? Fourteen? Do I hear fifteen?"

Candace Honeycluster launched her paddle toward her competitor, striking her square on the jaw. "Sold! For fifteen thousand dollars to the lady in the red jacket!"

The woman let out a shriek of joy and bellowed, "Never

fuck with Honeycluster!"

"If you liked that one, folks, hold onto your hats," gasped the auctioneer, "'cause here's another abstract by J. Glades, and it's a doozy."

The auctioneer wiped his brow and the audience members fanned themselves as the second canvas was placed upon the easel. It depicted Elvis and George Washinton high-fiving, surrounded by swirling colors. The crowd oohed and ahhed. "We'll be starting the bidding a bit higher on this one," said the auctioneer with a confident air. He couldn't believe what enormous sums these suckers would pay for something so incredibly odd. "Who will give me ten thousand?" he said, licking his lips.

# CHAPTER 32

In the candlelit glow of Joe Glades' cramped studio/home, Joe and Summer lay panting on a mat on the floor. They were covered with smears of multihued paint and bathed in sweat, staring at the ceiling, totally spent. The sex had been explosive, nothing like Summer had experienced with Dick Lance in furtive meetings in a dressing room or during an afternoon tryst at the Travelodge. The combination of intensity, power, and tenderness from this young man was like nothing she had ever felt. As for Joe, he was in a trance. As handsome as he was, his isolation, shyness and unorthodox upbringing had made sexual encounters few and far between.

Summer smiled at him and gently rubbed his chest. "Now that was an 'aha' moment."

The next day at breakfast, Joe and Summer were all over each other like a French art film. Mama Strongbow hummed a happy tune and pretended not to notice, relieved that Joe had actually found a partner.

Joe came up with a plan to impress Summer with something extra special. "What do you think about going to the beach?" he said.

"What beach? You mean that grody canal? Don't make me hurl."

"No, the real deal. The Atlantic Ocean. It's a bit of a drive, but let's get outta here and go swimming."

"I don't have a swimsuit."

"That's okay, we can drop by Walmart on the way."

"Terrif! That sounds spectac, plus, plus!"

They started out on the long drive east to the beach in Joe's Plymouth Duster, sitting close together in the way that newly minted lovebirds do. It was hot and sunny, a perfect beach day, and the couple held hands as they sped down the road. Joe pointed out wildlife when he could, but it was actually a deadly dull drive.

"Hey, look over there," he said. Two giant birds with huge beaks were pecking at the earth by the side of the road.

"Are those more herons?" asked Summer.

"Nope, they're cranes, sandhill cranes. People around

here call 'em white trash flamingos."

"Well, that's dumb-oh. They've got crazy big noses, though."

The wide-open spaces gave way to traffic lights, urban sprawl, and ticky-tacky strip malls. Summer began softly singing "Suddenly Symore" from Little Shop. Her hand slowly drifted down to Joe's thigh, and she began a gentle caress that made Joe suddenly forget about the beach. Soon he was dizzy with desire and had an urgent pounding in his brain. He began to grope Summer with feverish strokes. The fog of passion made the couple blind to the world around them and they made it as far as the perimeter road that encircles Palm Beach International airport. Joe pulled off onto a dirt road that disappeared into a clump of cabbage palms. The path led to a clearing along a chain link fence. More low trees on the other side of the fence meant this little clearing was totally secluded, a little oasis seemingly in the middle of nowhere. What they didn't know was that this patch of land was part of the "Clear Zone" for the approach to runway Ten Left at PBI.

Joe and Summer eagerly bounded out of the car and immediately clutched each other in a hot, sweaty embrace. This magical inner sanctum of nature seemed made just for them. Joe's shirt came off. Summer flung her clothes on the hood of the car in a mad rush. Joe hoisted her up on the left front fender of the Duster and dropped his jeans to his ankles. There was no one to hear their moans of ecstasy. The Duster rocked side to side. Their voices grew louder as they shouted each other's names. Gripped with passion, they had no sensory perception of the world around them. The rising note of rushing air. A growing, deafening, howling whine that both confused and thrilled them.

"This is amazing!" Joe shouted as Summer screamed, and he turned to see a Boeing 737 inbound from Atlanta passing three hundred feet over their heads, each window filled with an incredulous face staring down at their naked, thrusting bodies. The plane disappeared over the horizon, and the air grew suddenly silent. Joe and Summer were speechless.

"Well, that was different," Joe finally managed.

"True stor," panted Summer.

They hastily put their clothes back on and managed to drive away in the nick of time before airport security showed up. If they had bothered to check You-Tube, they could have found a number of cell phone videos of their escapade; luckily, no faces were visible.

The beach turned out to be anticlimactic, but very relaxing.

# CHAPTER 33

Leon Shively and Kristen had returned to his home in Lake Worth, giddy with the events of the evening at AArtistic Auction. The paintings had caused a near riot, and they felt lucky to sneak out without getting beaned by an overzealous art aficionado. Shiveley proposed they toast the good fortune of the newly crowned king of abstract art, Joe Glades, with a bottle of wine. He popped the cork on a pinot noir while Kristen sliced some brie without the aid of any new-fangled miracle gadget and arranged it on a tray with crackers at the small kitchen table.

"For the life of me, I can't figure out the excitement about those paintings," said Shively, savoring his first sip and breathing in the bouquet. "It just seems so random. It's as though somebody just squirted paint willy-nilly all over, like those spinning splatter paint things at the carnival when we were kids. Know what I mean?"

"Oh, I remember those. You got a little card that spun around and around, and you dribbled paint on it. My mom put it up on the refrigerator like it was the *Mona Lisa*." Kristen smiled at the recollection. "Well, I think Joe Glades puts a lot more of himself into his paintings than that."

Shively smacked his forehead. "Hey, that could be a million-dollar idea!" His eyes lit up and he licked his lips. "A direct-response splatter paint kit. It would be dirt cheap to make; the kids would love it. I can get little electric motors from Hong Kong for a quarter apiece. Batteries not included, of course."

"The parents would go insane with the cleanup."

"Ah, that's their problem." Shively took another hit of wine. "Wait, I've got it. You put the spinning card in the kitchen sink and use water-based paint. Cleanup's a breeze! I'll have to look into that. Needs a good name, though. Something magical. Maybe Splatter Magic. Perfect! I wonder if Joe Glades would do a testimonial?"

"I rather doubt it," said Kristen.

Shively let out a sigh. "I wish Dick were here to see all this. We had a lot of big sellers together. I'll never forget the incredible success of our weight loss product, Fatronic 2000. We had a fantastic shoot for that one. Big budget. Got some real porkers for the "before" shots, and some amazing babes for the "after" pictures and testimonials. Oh yeah, Dick had a lot of fun with that one."

Kristen shot him daggers. "Oh really?"

Shively quickly back-peddled. "Oh, what I mean is he really enjoyed the challenge of fine-tuning an exceptional commercial; it was like a Hollywood production. He was so talented. It hit big, too. Record-breaking sales. The fulfillment house could barely keep up with the orders. Everybody in the industry took notice.

Kristen frowned. "It may have been a big deal, but I don't remember hearing about that one at all."

Shively stared at his wine glass wistfully. "Well, yeah it was going gangbusters until, uh, well there were a few deaths."

Kristen's eyes widened in shock. "Deaths? As in people actually died from the stuff?"

"Yeah, just three or four, and they were probably in real bad shape anyway. Turns out there was a certain chemical used in horse racing that some people's systems couldn't handle. Hey, don't get me wrong, lots of people lost a ton of weight, but that company had to fold, cease, and desist, and the quack doctor who owned it went into hiding. He wound up in jail anyway when he was caught doing Brazilian butt lifts with Fix A Flat down in Hialeah."

Kristen's mind was spinning. Her eyes fell to the Mega Meal A Gizer sitting in the center of the kitchen table. "How soon before you hear about your new chopper?"

"Should be anytime now," replied Shively, draining his pinot noir. "My associates in Hong Kong think the world of me."

\*\*\*

Chin and Chan were dressed in black from head to toe. They were channeling their limited experience in martial arts. As teenagers, they had been thrown out of a tae kwon do class for bullying the other students. After that, anything they learned had come from kung fu movies and video games. They crept across Shively's lawn like ninjas on a bender. Wearing dark glasses was a bad idea. Chin stumbled into a fake flamingo, snapping one of its legs.

"Shut up!" hissed Chan, who dove to the ground as though he were hit with a stun gun. Inside the house, Leon and Kristen were oblivious. With the air conditioning on and Leon's double pane windows, they couldn't hear a thing outside. Chan wormed his way past some bushes and peeked into a window. He was stunned to see a fully lit Christmas tree. Then he noticed lights on in the kitchen and motioned Chin to circle around to the back of the house.

They carefully stuck their faces in the kitchen window to discover not just Kristen and Leon, but the fabled Mega Meal A Gizer itself. Shively fed an apple into the machine, and it disappeared in a blur, spitting out perfect uniform slices.

"It's the gizmo!" Chan exclaimed in an excited whisper. "We've finally got it!"

"Sssssh," whispered Chin, "Don't screw it up!"

Shively looked up at the window just as the two black ski mask-covered heads dropped out of sight. "You hear something?" he asked Kristen.

"Nope. Show me some more tricks with that thing; it sure has caused everyone a lot of heartbreak."

Shively produced a pepperoni sausage from the refrigerator and fed it into the machine. Quarter-sized slices of sausage cascaded out of the unit like a Las Vegas slot machine jackpot. Leon's eyebrows began to twitch excitedly. Suddenly, the kitchen door exploded inward with a thunderous sound and blinding billows of smoke. Chan had decided that real ninjas used explosives to open doors, just like the movies. Unfortunately, he'd miscalculated the amount of explosive to use, and he and Chin were knocked backwards off their feet into the koi pond as fish and frogs leaped for their lives.

Leon, being closest to the door, had been knocked unconscious by the blast and lay in a crumpled heap on the floor. Kristen was stunned, disoriented, and cut by flying glass. She sat frozen at the table, unable to make sense of what had just happened. A high-pitched squeal rang in her ears.

Suddenly, Chin and Chan lurched clumsily through the splintered doorway. They were wet, dirty, and bleeding from shrapnel wounds.

"Not you again," she sighed, unable to work up any real strength to run or scream.

"What?" croaked Chan, rubbing his ears. "Yeah, lady, it's us. We're repeat offenders."

"The Chinese surprise!" shouted Chin over the annoying squealing in his damaged eardrums. He half-heartedly mustered his ninja spirit. "Gimme that damn kitchen thing."

Kristen glowered at him and gave a shrug. "Go on; take it. It doesn't matter. There will be a new version of it on the market in three weeks."

"Oh, really?" said Chin loudly, "Well, you may be surprised to know that order has been cancelled."

"What do you mean, cancelled?" asked Kristen, rubbing her eyes and becoming more fully aware.

"Your buddy here ain't so smart. He put in an order to knock off this gadget with the same company that made the damn thing in the first place. Ain't that somethin', old man?" Chin leaned over Shively's body and shouted. "Hey old man, you hear me? You fucked up. Hey, what's wrong with him?"

Kristen knelt down to Leon, feeling for a pulse. There was none. "You bastards!" she screamed. "You killed him! You killed him for a lousy piece of junk! A fucking kitchen chopper!"

Chin pulled off his ski mask as the enormity of the situation sank in. "Gee, we didn't mean to hurt nobody."

Chan smacked Chin's shoulder. "What kind of ninja takes off his mask?"

"It doesn't matter, you moron. I've seen both your faces, and I'll never forget them," said Kristen bitterly.

Chan picked up the Mega Meal A Gizer and motioned to Chin.

"You know what? She's right. We got a stiff on our hands. This is serious shit. She can I.D. us. I don't fuckin' believe it. We gotta take her with us."

Kristen let out a groan. "Not again."

# CHAPTER 34

As the ambulance took away the shroud-covered body of Leon Shively, Sheriff's Deputy Russell examined the blown-out kitchen. A technician dusted for fingerprints. Photos were taken. The whole house was searched. Russell was both relieved and worried to find no sign of Kristen. He noticed a number of pepperoni slices scattered throughout the debris. "Must have been making a killer of a pizza," he mused out loud. A crime scene technician handed Russell a wet wad of paper that he had fished out of the koi pond. It was a bag with a logo from Lee Ho's Szechuan Palace containing one soggy crab rangoon that had fallen from Chin's pocket. Captain Block angrily pushed his way through the splintered door.

"Russell, what the hell is going on with this case? Now we have a murder? What is this? Amateur hour? Have you been wasting away in Parrotville, or do you have any clue what this is all about?"

"I'm on it, Captain," he snapped. "Kristen Lance—er—Daniels—has been taken hostage again. I'm guessing it's the Asian thugs that grabbed her before."

"Unbelievable! What the hell is wrong with you? How could you let this happen? I thought you were watching her. You call yourself an officer of the law?"

"I thought she was in good hands," he said, bitterly. "Obviously not. We're gonna find her. I've got a pretty good idea where they might be holed up," He carefully pocketed the damp Chinese take-out bag. "I'm heading over to the skid row area by the Raw. I need some undercover backup. No showboats, no Starsky or Hutch. I'll find her."

"You fuck this up, and you'll be doing security at Walmart for the rest of your life! Got it?" Captain Block spat on the floor to punctuate his statement.

"Nice," said Russell, trying to control his temper as he stepped carefully out of the crumbling kitchen. "Now your DNA is on the crime scene."

\*\*\*

After the catastrophic explosion, the stunned ninjas had stuffed Kristen, bound and gagged, into the back seat of their car and driven aimlessly, ears ringing, brains throbbing, in search of a drug store. Chan was in no shape to drive. He was totally lost and carelessly took out a stop sign while driving fifty yards down a sidewalk, which luckily was empty.

"Dude, stop!" shouted Chin, "You're gonna kill us all."

"My bad," grumbled Chan. "Gimme a minute." With the car idling, he searched through his pockets and found two Percocets, popping them both in his bloody mouth and washing them down with a swig of beer. "That's better," he grunted. "Now where are we?"

"Man, where did you learn about explosives?" asked Chin.

"On the internet, of course. I guess I shouldn't have put in an extra pinch of gunpowder for good luck."

"Yeah, some luck. Get back onto the street before somebody sees us."

After a few deep breaths, Chan pulled back onto the street. He motored on a little more carefully, finally finding a CVS pharmacy. Chan got out to shoplift some bandages while Chin waited in the car, motor running, with Kristen imprisoned in the back. Chin turned to face her, his face registering true regret.

"I'm really sorry about all this," he stammered. "And I'm so sorry about your friend. Major bummer. This ain't what we had in mind when we got this job. This is totally screwed up."

Kristen stared intently at her captor. She tried to speak, but it was futile with the gag in her mouth. Chin continued to explain that they really weren't the bad guys they seemed.

"We're just tryin' to make a livin'. It ain't easy. Like, we got a raw deal. Hey, my name's Jerry by the way, and Chan's first name is Norbert." He gave a half-hearted chuckle. "I know, right? Maybe that's what makes him so mean."

Kristen stared in silence as her blood boiled. In the CVS, the cashier was distracted by an older lady wearing a red ball cap who insisted on getting her money back for an "As Seen on

TV!" item. The cashier stubbornly shook her head.

"I'm sorry, ma'am, but there don't be any refunds on those; you gotta send it back to the manufacturer."

"Is that so?" roared Candace Honeycluster. "This thing exploded like a suicide bomber in my microwave and shot crap all over my kitchen! Somebody's going to pay!"

The cashier was not impressed. "You can take it up with the manager tomorrow, but you'll just be wastin' your time."

"We'll see," sneered Candace, heading to the back of the store where the "As Seen on TV!" shelf was located. In seconds, smoke began to rise from the display as flames engulfed a box of chamois wipes that were touted to "soak up liquid like a thirsty camel." The cashier noticed the billowing smoke and started screaming, yanking on the fire alarm. In the following chaos, the bloodied shoplifter was never noticed, and the kidnappers were long gone when Candace Honeycluster stomped out of the store shouting, "Nobody fucks with Honeycluster!"

***

Chan steered the dark sedan into a parking lot by a check-cashing store, and the two men took turns clumsily wrapping each other in bandages. They looked like extras from a zombie apocalypse movie. Chin turned around and gingerly put a band-aid on a cut on Kristen's forehead and announced to Chan he had had enough. He wanted to dump Kristen on an empty street corner and head home. Chan exploded with obscenities and declared the subject closed. His mood had turned beyond dark. Regaining his bearings, he pointed the car back toward Lee Ho's, where they blindfolded and tied up Kristen in their tiny apartment, scanning the ceiling for attic access. Neither man felt even remotely like a ninja.

# CHAPTER 35

On a dark, depressing street on the forgotten side of Riviera Beach, Chief Billy, now wearing a pullover and cargo pants to be incognito, along with his two henchmen Skinny Sal and Vito, who wore Hawaiian shirts, had camped out in the Escalade. They had seen no sign of Kristen or the Asian kidnappers, but they had been approached by four drug dealers, two hookers, and a guy who wanted to sell them stolen stereo speakers.

"That's without a doubt the cheapest blowjob I've ever been offered," sighed Billy. "Can you believe it? Five bucks."

"The speakers weren't bad," offered Skinny Sal.

"I wouldn't trust a hummer in this neighborhood," said Vito.

"Count me out. I can't do that kinda thing anymore," Sal said wistfully.

"Yeah, well I'm a happily married man," said Billy.

"That's not what I mean. It don't work."

"What don't work?"

"It," said Sal ruefully. "Thanks for bringin' up the subject." There was an awkward pause.

"Um. Sorry. Let's try a different street." "I still say we just go door-to-door bustin' heads," griped Vito.

Billy gave Vito a scowl, doubting that this over-the-hill gang of geezers could strike fear into anybody. He started the big Caddy and slowly rolled down the block. He took a right and discovered Lee Ho's Szechuan Palace two hundred yards away. "Woah, now we're getting' somewhere. I got a good feelin' about this. I say we get ourselves some chop suey," said Billy.

The trio couldn't have looked more out of place as they pushed through the front door of the restaurant. The lighting was dim with paper lanterns hung on the red walls. They found an empty booth and seated themselves before the hostess could reach them. An attractive Asian woman approached them with menus in her hand. "Three for dinner?" she asked.

"Just some snacks, uh, Sugar Blossom," said Billy. "Maybe some egg rolls and wonton soup."

"Hey, you have miso soup? Miso horny," snickered Vito.

Without missing a beat, the waitress said," Okay, order of egg rolls. Two wonton. One miso soup. Oh, and our special today is Sum Dim Jerk. Something to drink?"

Billy and Skinny Sal rolled their eyes at Vito's offensive attempt at humor and ordered a round of beers.

"Don't mind him, dear," said Billy. "He don't get out much." The three drank beers for a little over an hour, one after the other, constantly scanning the room for the kidnappers.

Finally, Vito asked the waitress, "Hey, have you seen a couple of really funny lookin' Chinese guys around here?"

"What do you mean by funny?" asked the waitress, who had had just about enough of these creeps. "Don't we all look alike?"

"Well, yeah, but these guys are particularly strange."

"Yeah, no offense, they're bad apples. Ninja gangster types," said Billy.

"As you can see," the waitress said coolly, "everyone in here is Asian, the customers are Asian, the staff is Asian. The dishwashers are Asian. You tell me who looks strange, old man."

"Well, uh, hey," said Billy, "We don't mean to…" He froze in mid-sentence. Across the room, Chin and Chan, conspicuous in their bandages and gauze from the explosion, were walking cautiously into the room from the back door. "It's them!" shouted Billy. "The Blues Brothers!"

He lunged clumsily from his seat, knocking over plates and utensils with a clatter. The kidnappers immediately made an about face and disappeared out the back as the mob trio struggled to free themselves from their booth. They were stuck.

A sweaty man with a chef's hat lurched from the kitchen and began shouting in Mandarin, banging on a pot like a gong. The waitress hauled off and whacked Vito hard with a serving tray as he tried to pass by. "Now I Dim Sum old guy," she smirked.

A sea of personnel, desperate to escape, came pouring out of the kitchen, into the hallway, and out the back door. Busboys, waitresses, and patrons stampeded past the mob trio.

In the chaos Billy, Vito, and Skinny Sal cowered in fear at the thought of actually confronting dozens of angry immigrants who were much younger and more athletic than themselves.

\*\*\*

Just at that moment Mike Russell and his undercover backup unit pulled up, spotting the Cadillac Escalade outside of Lee Ho's. They screeched to a stop, then heard the mayhem. Russell and his team sprang from their cars and charged into the restaurant with weapons drawn. "Police!" he shouted. "Don't anybody move."

The effect of the order was just the opposite. The remaining patrons jumped over tables and chairs like acrobats on speed, sprang out the back door, and vanished into the night. Suddenly, the place was totally quiet. Only the three aging mobsters were left in a disheveled heap on the floor surrounded by scattered rice, wontons, and crushed fortune cookies.

"Some detectives you guys turned out to be," said Russell dryly. "I told you to keep your noses out of this."

"We was just tryin' to help," said Billy, picking himself up and wiping off some egg foo young. "But we saw them. The kidnappers. They were right here! Those guys got to be around here somewhere with the lady. Somewhere real close."

Two more sheriff's cars lurched to a halt outside the restaurant, and four deputies charged in with guns drawn.

"Easy guys, there's nothing left but Chinese takeout." Russell said," Go through the building and see if there are any stragglers. Search everywhere."

After going room-to-room, through the kitchen, the supply room, janitor's closet, restrooms, and searching the back premises, the deputies found no one. Not a cook, busboy, or waitress, let alone a pair of would-be ninja kidnappers.

"I'll bet there wasn't a U.S. citizen in the whole place," grumbled Billy. "If you hadn't showed up, we would have taken care of those guys. It would've been easy. They look like pure shit. They got bloody bandages like they were in a car wreck."

"Bandages? Thanks for the tip," said Mike. "Now, you guys are under arrest."

"What for?"

"Obstruction of justice, aggravated assault, inciting a riot, that's enough to hold you a little while. Take them away, boys."

"What about our rental Cadillac?" whined Vito, "It'll get trashed here. I got a deposit on it."

"One of the deputies will drive it to headquarters. Hey, it's for your own good, Chief. I have to get you guys out of my hair so I can do my job."

***

Mike sat back behind the wheel of his unmarked car contemplating what to do next. He knew that despite their bungling, the hapless mobsters and the crazy Indian were right. The kidnappers couldn't be too far away.

Mike obsessed about Kristen and realized that beyond just doing his job trying to find a kidnap victim, he had gone off the deep end. He started the car and motored slowly around the block toward the rear of the restaurant and the adjoining apartments. In the dark trash-strewn street a slim figure walked slowly, head down, studying the sidewalk. He pulled up alongside and lowered the window. The shuffling woman was wearing torn blue jeans and a Rolling Stones T-shirt. It was Wheezy. Everyone in the Sheriff's Department knew Wheezy. The old addict noticed the car and perked up, striding up to Mike Russell's window, then her face fell, realizing this wasn't a possible trick.

"Howdy, Officer," she rasped. "Nice night, ain't it?

"Yeah, Wheezy, nice night. See anything?"

"I'm not doin' nothin', just walkin', lookin' for loose change, half-smoked butts, you know." Her fingers twitched and she avoided eye contact, staring at the dirty pavement.

"Don't worry, I'm not accusing you of anything. I just want to know if you've seen anything suspicious tonight. I'm looking for a couple of Chinese thugs."

Wheezy let out a cackling laugh that reverberated off a nearby building. "You come to the right neighborhood for Chinese guys. This is like Beijing without the bicycles."

# CHAPTER 36

Chin and Chan had rushed back to the dingy apartment where Kristen was tied tightly to a chair, blindfolded, a gag covering her mouth. They quickly untied her feet and released her from the chair but left her hands bound and her mouth covered. Chin opened the door a few inches and peered out into the now deserted street. Seeing no one, the two henchmen pushed and pulled Kristen outside and hustled her into the back seat of their newly stolen Ford sedan. One block away, Mike Russell was talking with Wheezy the street walker, who mentioned she had just seen two highly suspicious men covered in bandages run into an apartment down the block.

Chan started the car and pulled around the corner, gaining speed past a scruffy woman talking to a man in a car. "Guess that guy's about to get laid," he commented as he accelerated away from the scene, weaving slightly. He turned to look at the pathetic figure of Kristen bundled in the back seat and mumbled to Chin through his bandages, "I don't see why we shouldn't get lucky too, know what I'm sayin?"

Chin got the sinking feeling that with all that had happened his partner had lost his mind. "I dunno, man. Aren't ninjas supposed to be above that sort of thing?"

Chan gave a snort, his words starting to slur, "We're ninjas, not Knights of the fuckin' Round Table."

They drove in silence for a few minutes, headed east out of the gritty area of town, but then turned south on Broadway, passing a variety of marine service shops, gas stations, and liquor stores, directly toward the Port of Palm Beach. Chin popped a beer, took a sip, then with a sigh pressed the cold metal can to his forehead to ease the throbbing. The explosion had sent shards of glass into his right temple, which was oozing blood from under the clumsy layer of bandages.

Chan had fallen backwards and hit his head on the concrete edge of the koi pond in Leon Shively's backyard. The fall gave him a nasty gash that, in any emergency room, would have required stitches. It also gave him a throbbing, colossal headache and the sudden twisted notion that he was the victim. He had felt disadvantaged all his life, and now he should get his just reward.

Rising up in the distance at the Port, like a Disney World apparition, a brightly lit cruise ship dazzled in the night, beckoning passengers to a fun-filled, sun-soaked vacation in the Bahamas. The stolen Ford was not headed to the festive passenger terminal. This was no dream vacation. The sedan turned away from the brightly lit fantasy scene and toward the dark cargo holding area.

*** 

A rising tide of panic began to grip Kristen with the force of an Everglades python. The two kidnappers had always seemed more like bungling goofballs than sadistic creeps. Neither one had ever tried to harm her even when they had the opportunity. She feared something had changed. She urgently replayed memories of her father's self-defense lessons from when she was a young woman. Pokes to the eyes, a chop to the throat, a kick to the crotch. She toyed with the idea of flinging herself out of the car, providing she could even get the door open, but realized it would be foolish if not fatal.

The stolen Ford slowed as it entered the drab, industrial Port of Palm Beach storage complex, past rows of parked semis and shipping containers from around the world. It came to a stop at an imposing cargo gate marked No Trespassing Authorized Personnel Only. Chan gave a hand signal. The watchman in the guardhouse recognized the gesture, and the tall chain link gate began to creak noisily open. Once inside the gate, Chin stopped the car and watched it rattle closed behind them. He took another swig of beer and chuckled, "Now that's what I call Homeland Security. Finally, we can relax. So, which container is supposed to be the secret hideout?"

Perhaps it was the excruciating headaches and blurred vision combined with Percocet and beer that caused the inept ninjas to not notice they had been followed all the way from the Raw to the Port. Mike Russell had noticed the suspicious car accelerating past him as he talked to Wheezy. He tailed them, keeping a discreet distance behind. He had already called for backup. He paused for a moment by the side of the road to let assistance catch up, and he lit up the red and blue flashing lights concealed in the grill and rear window of his car.

"That one, right there," said Chan. It's got a monkey paw symbol on the door."

Chin pulled the car to a stop in front of the container. He got out and struggled to open the heavy metal door, then jumped back and let out a disgusted groan.

"Holy shit! That's some skank stank! Dude, this container hideout idea ain't gonna fly. We can't stay in this cesspool. No way!"

He held his hand to his mouth as Chan wrestled Kristen Daniels, kicking and cursing, out of the backseat of the Ford. He finally got her out of the car and dragged her into the fetid container. Kristen tried to catch a glimpse through the blindfold she was wearing but couldn't make out a thing in the dark, dank confines of the container.

All she knew was the smell was unbearable. The commingled odors of sweat, urine, blood, and excrement made her suddenly feel ill. She screamed into the gag in her mouth as loudly as she could, the sound reverberating off the metal walls.

"Shut up!" hissed Chan. "Nobody can hear you. There's nobody around here but us. This is a quarantine area. No-Man's-Land. Nobody can come or go unless they're with us. Know what I'm sayin?"

He shoved Kristen down roughly onto a rickety chair. He was dripping sweat, his eyes blinking wildly. "This dump ain't perfect, but it's time to get some payback for all our trouble. And lady, believe me, you've been nothing but trouble," he said through labored breathing. "Help me retie her hands behind her back, Chin."

"Aw, c'mon man! You're out of your mind! We've got the gadget, let's just leave her and get the hell outta here. This is nuts. You're gonna ruin everything!"

"At this point, I figure there's nothin' to lose. Grab her, dammit."

"Asshole. This is not the ninja way."

Kristen struggled with all her might as the two men held her arms. She managed to get one arm free and swung blindly, slamming Chin square in the groin. He groaned, doubled over in pain and dropped to the floor with a metallic thud.

Chan grappled for control of her arms, but by now her blindfold had slipped from her eyes, and she could make out the menacing figure in front of her. She gave her best karate kick and sent Chan sprawling onto the filthy floor of the container. He was momentarily stunned, but powered by rage, he sprang up and gave her a hard slap across the face. Despite having ingested enough booze and pills to drop a rhino, he succeeded in loosely tying her hands behind her back, but instead of fastening her to the chair, he stood her up in a bear hug and yanked her like a rag doll out of the container and toward the Ford.

"Okay, the container was a dumbass idea," he growled; then, his voice softened. "Hey, c'mon, everybody loves a ninja, right? There's somethin' magic and mysterious about us. It's that bad-boy thing. Try to relax." He shoved her onto the rear seat of the Ford, and she fell backward like a broken puppet.

Chan fumbled with his pants, then clumsily launched himself on top of her, ham-fistedly ripping at her clothes. She fought back like a cornered animal, kicking and writhing. The bloody bandage around Chans' head flopped down, obscuring his vision, and in his lust-filled, drugged haze, he never noticed that Kristen had worked her right hand free of its poorly tied bonds.

"Norbert! Kristen screamed through her gag, "Stop, Norbert! Just stop!"

Chan froze for a second, dumbfounded at the sound of his own name. A name he despised. Kristen grabbed the Mega Meal A Gizer off the floor of the car with her free hand and switched it on. It sprang to life with a whir as she pressed it to her attacker, and being set to "crush" it began to chop ice cube-sized pieces of flesh out of Chan. He reared up in pain, and Kristen jabbed the hungry Mega Meal A Gizer frantically at his body, ripping bloody divots that would make Jack the Ripper thoroughly jealous.

His gurgling scream echoed through the storage yard as he fell backward out of the car and smashed heavily to the asphalt in a ghastly heap, cracking his skull even further. He lay motionless as the whirring Mega Meal A Gizer spun in circles next to him. Kristen's vision began to blur as she thought to herself, "That's one for Leon. Crushes nuts with ease, and cleanup's a breeze." She fainted dead away.

No sooner had Kristen passed out in the back seat of the Ford than dozens of agents and police streamed in, surrounding the scene. ICE, FBI, CBP, Marine patrol, Coast Guard, and Palm Beach County Sheriff cars with sirens wailing all jockeyed for position to take part in the big bust.

"Wow! That guy looks like he was attacked by a wolverine!" said one wide-eyed Sheriff's deputy, eyeing the bloodied body of Chan and self-consciously covering his own groin. The injured ninja wannabe was loaded into an ambulance and spirited away. Chin popped his head out of the container door like a frightened squirrel and froze, wondering what Bruce Lee would do. He gave a feeble ninja war cry that was more of a squeak and immediately surrendered. A half dozen cops with guns drawn and adrenaline pumping yelled, "On the ground now!" He dropped flat on the ground, face down, and was handcuffed and hauled away in a very un-ninja-like fashion.

# CHAPTER 37

Surveillance cameras had clearly caught Candace Honeycluster in the act of setting fire to the CVS pharmacy's "As Seen On TV!" display. The fire alarm sounded as she marched out the door in righteous rage. When the officers appeared at her apartment door a few hours later to take her into custody, they thought this little old lady would meekly submit, and they would quietly take her to jail. Instead, she began to kick and curse and scratch like a Tasmanian devil. A local news team covering the arrest caught the outrageous action on video.

"Nobody fucks with Honeycluster!" she screamed repeatedly in a fountain of spittle. "Police brutality! I'll sue you all!" She took a swipe at the cameraman, and the expensive camera tumbled to the ground.

That night on Live Action News Now, the whole scene was broadcast at both six and eleven. Curse words were discreetly bleeped, and the news team had a good laugh.

Charged with attempted arson and resisting arrest, she bonded out of jail only to be met by a small crowd of enthusiastic supporters wearing red hats and chanting "Free Honeycluster!" Some carried signs reading "Nobody F*cks With Honeycluster!" The footage of the event went viral and even appeared on FOX.

Candy Honeycluster was flabbergasted to find that a Go Fund Me site had been set up for her legal defense, and people were contributing money at a fast clip. Local movers and shakers were encouraging her to run for City Commission. Within a few days she held a press conference in front of the very same CVS she had torched. She was flanked by rabid supporters waving her signature slogan.

"Tell us, ma'am, what is your platform if you are elected?" asked reporter Katisha Merryweather somberly, holding out a microphone.

"I'm gonna kick butt and take names, puppet media lady! I'm no politician, and that's my strength." The crowd hooted and roared approval. "I'm gonna put the people first. I'm gonna come in like a big enema and flush all the assholes out of office one by one!"

"And what about the serious charges against you for arson and resisting arrest?"

"Fake news! A bunch of B.S.! That's not gonna hold up in court; that was spontaneous combustion! Now who wants to make a campaign contribution?" Indeed, with a proper amount of behind-the-scenes palm greasing from opaque political action committees, the charges were dropped, and Candace Honeycluster was duly elected to the Palm Beach City Commission.

# CHAPTER 38

A quiet hospital room materialized before her eyes as Kristen regained consciousness. She struggled to focus. There were flowers in a small vase on a nightstand. An IV drip was attached to her right wrist with a clear fluid running through a tube. A monitor displayed heartbeat and blood pressure. Her vision was blurry, and she felt woozy. She closed her eyes again, trying to return to some dream with a better ending than this. She drifted back to sleep, but the dream was not what she had hoped for. She saw her hospital room in sharper detail. The TV set mounted on the wall had a close-up of a woman staring in horror into a mirror. A voiceover announcer spoke. It was the bombastic voice of Dick Lance.

"Are you tired of all those wrinkles making you look older than you really are?" A big red "X" covered the woman's face. She cringed in exaggerated shame. "Not anymore! Introducing Essence of Escargot! The concentrated snail extract that tightens and rejuvenates your skin like magic! Just look at this before and after comparison."

Side-by-side pictures showed the woman as an impossibly wrinkled old hag and a youthful, smooth-skinned beauty. Kristen recognized the woman. It was the voluptuous Verushka, Dick's most recent talent discovery. His voice implored, "French women have known this secret beauty regimen for years; now it can be yours!" Verushka smiled at the camera and gave her best stab at a French accent.

"C'est magnifique!" she gushed, with a trace of Russian.

"But wait; there's more!" shouted over-the-top Dick Lance.

Verushka froze, looking puzzled. She frowned off-camera. "You say butt weight?"

"But wait, there's more, it's a figure of speech."

"My butt!" Verushka burst into tears. "You call me fat ass!" she sobbed.

Kristen abruptly awoke from her nightmare shouting, "But wait! But wait!" Mike Russell was seated by her side, wearing a Hawaiian shirt and a bemused smile.

"But what are we waiting for? Hallelujah, she's alive!"

He held her hand.

"Mike, what am I doing here? I just had the weirdest dream." She reached out to touch his face.

"You got pretty banged up. Concussion, fractured ribs, you put up quite a fight."

"You should see the other guy."

"Believe me, I did."

*** 

A few weeks after her ordeal, Kristen's cuts and bruises were mostly healed, and she had taken up temporary residence at Mike Russell's Lake Worth home. The ex-wife's closet was cleared out of old memories, and Mike was no longer relegated to sleeping on the couch. The Mega Meal A Gizer was impounded as evidence, which was fine with Kristen. She never wanted to see it again.

Chin and Chan were brought up on charges of kidnapping, assault, drug possession, weapons violations, and auto theft, among other items. Their public defender pointed to their being bullied in school, as well as their poor upbringing and over-exposure to violent kung fu movies at a tender age, but the judge was not impressed. It turned out they had warrants for their arrest in New Jersey on fraud and burglary charges as well as public urination. They were denied bail and sent straight to jail where they could practice their martial arts to their heart's content.

Kristen thought from time to time about Dick Lance with very mixed feelings. Through a specially expedited ruling assisted by the Palm Beach Sheriff's department and a friendly judge with substantial clout, he was now declared legally deceased, and the investment firm of Randolph, Grayson, and Gleason confirmed that she was the rightful beneficiary of his investment portfolio. She transferred the money into an account in her own name, deciding not to rush into what to do with it, but she now felt empowered like never before.

Kristen had insisted on taking Mike out for a celebratory dinner on her own dime. They had unanimously decided against Chinese food and settled on a romantic French place overlooking the broad waters of Lake Worth. The lights of yachts reflected on the calm water as a bright moon rose in the east over the mansions of Palm Beach. A gray-haired pianist wearing a tuxedo played subdued French tunes on a baby grand in the corner of the room. A dashingly handsome waiter with an outrageous accent gave impeccable service. The meal was superb, but conversation was minimal. Neither one could put more than a few words together. It wasn't a case of not having anything to say, but too much. Unanswered questions crowded their thoughts. Kristen knew something was weighing on Mike's mind, and he could tell something was on hers. Finally, he wiped his mouth with his napkin, cleared his throat, and looked up from his chicken cordon bleu with a cautious smile.

"Uh, Kristen, I think we make a really good team."

She said nothing, pretending to need an immediate sip of wine. His words hung still in the air like a soap bubble about to pop. He looked down at his plate and poked his food in desperation. She reached out to touch his hand. He continued awkwardly.

"I've done a lot of thinking since the divorce. I was angry then. I was disappointed. But now I realize that, well, just maybe I was a disappointment too. Hard to believe, huh? I wasn't around enough. Not attentive enough." He swallowed hard. "Ok, I was a parrothead jerk and an overzealous crime fighter, but I know I can do better. I've thought about you, well, constantly, ever since we met. You're the strongest woman I've ever known. You're amazing. And hey, Rocket really likes you." The dog poked his furry snout out from beneath the tablecloth.

"Now that's romantic. Are you trying to deputize me?"

"Don't answer now; just think it over. I've got time, but I'm not getting any younger. Sooner or later my check engine light is going to come on."

"Your warranty is expiring?"

"I mean, I'm just a cop, but I've got a good feeling about you. I don't want to lose you. "

She looked into his eyes and smiled. "Frankly, I've got a thing for cops. And I've got time, too. Lots of time. But this is a hell of a lot to adjust to. I realize now that I rushed into my relationship with Dick way too fast. I thought he might be my last chance. It seems so silly. So sad. I've been through a painful wall of crap. I need to go home." Mike's eyes drifted down to his plate. "Sure, I understand."

"However," said Kristen with a sly grin, "First, take me to Key West. I think we should go to the Randy Rooster."

He broke into a relieved smile. "I do have a lot of vacation time coming."

# CHAPTER 39

On their way out of town they made a point to pass through the depressing neighborhood of the Raw, searching for Beauregard Street. Mike pulled over in front of the bleak apartment at 731½. In the light of day, it looked dingier than ever.

"Are you sure you want to do this? You could get Legionnaires' Disease in there."

Kristen didn't hesitate. "Absolutely. That little woman was an actual lifesaver." She kicked aside some bags of garbage on the sidewalk and knocked on the door. There was no answer, but the door was unlocked. She made her way inside the chaotic trash mound of a room and found Wheezy asleep on the couch with a bag of French fries on her lap. Kristen took an envelope filled with more cash than Wheezy had ever seen and gently slipped it under the worn blanket draped over her bony frame. A short note in the envelope would explain how thankful Kristen was for her kindness. She glanced once more around the room, gave a sad sigh, tiptoed out, and quietly shut the door.

Mike got onto the Florida Turnpike and headed south for the long drive to Key West. Naturally, Jimmy Buffett music from the car stereo set the mood. Key Largo signaled the beginning of the necklace of islands, with a non-stop parade of souvenir shops, bait and tackle stores, t-shirt shops, and seafood restaurants advertising bottomless margaritas. The beautiful vistas of the Overseas Highway lived up to their magical reputation, giving the illusion of driving off the end of the earth, but traffic was heavy on US-1.

All went smoothly until the island known as Islamorada. A jack-knifed boat trailer carrying a go-fast boat with four huge outboard motors blocked the southbound lanes. The truck towing the trailer had run a red light and smacked a van hauling a trailer full of rental canoes. The boat was leaning off the trailer at a crazy angle, and what looked like a bag full of Christmas presents had spilled onto the highway. Traffic came to a standstill, and people swarmed the packages like ants to a picnic. Mike and Kristen squinted into the distance to see what was going on. They watched in amazement as opportunists bolted from their cars and brazenly stuffed neatly wrapped packages of cocaine under their shirts. A fight broke out between two men wearing flip flops and swimsuits who started slugging each other while holding on to a brick of coke. Florida Highway Patrol cars came screaming up to the scene, and the scavengers rushed back to their cars trying to look nonchalant. The driver of the monster truck that was towing the boat was long gone.

"Wow, just another day in the Keys?" asked Kristen.

"I saw an awful lot of that in the Coast Guard," sighed Mike. "Hey, I'm off duty and out of jurisdiction. I know nothing."

*** 

The weekend at the Randy Rooster proved to be both the soothing and invigorating therapy they had been hoping for. The rickety old building that Mike remembered had been completely revamped with every luxury accommodation, including Jacuzzi tub and decadent fuzzy bathrobes and slippers. The sunset celebration at Mallory Square was a feast for the senses, complete with a fire eater, a mystic Swami who walked through broken glass, and a wild-eyed man who literally juggled cats while telling dirty cat jokes. A lady dressed as a mime was brazenly selling Jello shots from a cooler, doing a brisk business.

After a wickedly delicious lobster dinner at the Turtle Kralls, they returned to their room at the Rooster and opened a bottle of wine.

"Let's check conditions for snorkeling tomorrow," said Mike, pressing the remote to the enormous flat screen. He scrolled to a channel featuring weather, but only caught the tail end of the report. A commercial came on instead. Against a dark background, the words, "You don't have to suffer anymore," appeared on the screen. Tense music played, and a dramatic voice that sounded strangely familiar to Kristen spoke.

"In these troubled times, we all need help," said the voice emphatically. The screen changed to an elderly man looking confused. A distraught mother holding a crying baby. A young couple looking at a document with a giant stamp spelling, "EVICTED."

"Now, help is just a phone call away! 'With Elixir of Life Holy Oil'!" The music filled to a crescendo. A display of small bottles lit with dramatic effect filled the screen.

"You've got to be kidding me," scowled Mike, muting the volume.

"Wait," said Kristen, "That voice, turn it up." Mike cranked the sound as pictures of people joyously dabbing their foreheads, their pets, their children, and even their cars with the mysterious liquid flashed across the screen. A hapless driver was overjoyed when his beater car started with a roar. An elderly lady in a wheelchair stood up and began dancing like a maniac.

"This is your chance to change your life!" urged the announcer. "Get your bottle of holy oil! Go to our website, or call the number on your screen NOW!"

"It's him!" said Kristen. "It's Dick. He's putting on a dramatic weird thing with his voice, but it's him. I'm sure of it."

Mike was skeptical. ""You're really sure? You think it's recent? Or could he have recorded this some time ago?"

"Well, yes, definitely, I didn't know everything he was into. Maybe he was too embarrassed about this piece of crap."

"I would think so. Holy oil? More like snake oil. That's the lowest of the low," said Mike. "Can we *not* think about old Dick right now?"

Kristen snuggled up to Mike and said softly, "Absolutely. Turn off the damn TV."

"Ten four, it may be time for that game of good cop, bad cop."

# Chapter 40

Kristen and Mike made one last visit to the Alligator Outpost. The road signs beckoned with their taunting messages, "Live Baby Gators! Ice Cold Beer! Last Chance Gas!" As they turned in to the familiar sunbaked parking lot, they noticed a surprising number of improvements. The concrete teepees all had a fresh coat of paint. The Outpost Cafe had a new sign with a neon pot of coffee lit in 1950s splendor. A large banner with a comical cartoon of a smiling gator rippled in the wind. Kristen took Mike's hand in hers and sighed. "Y'know I'm going to miss this weird place. Not! But I owe so much to these folks."

They found the ex-mobster Indian and his charming wife standing out by the unusually crowded bleachers just as the alligator wrestling demonstration was winding down. Joe Glades, dressed in full Indian garb, was crouched over the thoroughly stoned-out-of-his-mind alligator, "Old Big Mouth," holding the toothy jaws open wide as Summer Springfield, ravishing in a buckskin bikini, fearlessly put her head inside the massive gator's gaping maw. Kids screamed, and the tourists gasped and applauded. Cell phones sprang up out of the crowd for pictures. One hapless young man whose pants were halfway down his butt ran up for a selfie, clumsily slipped on the wet pond deck, and did a pratfall into the water. The gator was nonplussed, but the audience went apeshit.

Billy crowed through the loudspeaker, "Ladies and gentlemen, make some noise for Miss Summer Springfield! Super-duper, Plus Plus!

"Well, what do you know?" thought Kristen, "Summer Springfield has finally made it big in show business."

Always the huckster, Chief Billy invited the audience into the gift shop. When the customers had all disappeared into the shop, the final goodbye was bittersweet.

"The money you brought in from my paintings has made a huge difference in fixin' this place up," said Joe Glades. "And I've got a bunch of orders from the auction house. Talk about a game changer. We couldn't have done it without you, ma'am. And I never would have met Summer, either."

Summer giggled and gave Joe a squeeze. "True stor,"

she said. "I have no guams about this handsome guy."

"You mean qualms?"

"Whatever."

"You really love me?" asked Joe.

Summer screwed up her cute little nose, "Don't be redic."

"Kristen you're like the daughter I never had; we're going to miss you around here. Bring it in!" said Billy as he locked her in a bear hug.

"You take care of yourself," said Mama, her bright eyes twinkling. "Watch out for those fast-talking TV salesmen, you hear? Oh, and just one thing before you go. Come with me back to the zoo. Just a few minutes. It's a special day."

Mama Strongbow had a smile on her face, and she hummed a cheery tune as Kristen and Mike followed her out back, down the path to the shady live oak that sheltered all the animal cages. Kristen could immediately feel the temperature cool down by a few degrees.

"Just look at this tree, Mike." said Kristen. "It's hundreds of years old. Look at those branches and all the beautiful Spanish moss."

"Amazing," he said, staring up at the massive tree. "Reminds me of ZZ Top."

The animals all perked up expectantly, clucking and bleating, looking for a handout, but Mama went straight to the big cage housing the red-tailed hawk.

"It's time for Red to try his wings."

The big bird eyed her suspiciously as she pulled on a pair of leather gloves, opened the cage door, and stepped back. Everyone held their breath as the bird considered the open door and shook his feathers. He hopped to the floor of the cage, gave one last look around, jumped through the opening, and vaulted for freedom. On a gust of wind, he effortlessly soared over their heads as shouts of awe sprang from the little gathering.

"He's good as new," said Mama, wrapping an arm around Kristen.

"So beautiful," said Kristen softly, the hawk shrinking

in the distance. "He's free!"

Within moments his mate appeared, and together they vanished into the distance.

\*\*\*

Driving away from the Alligator Outpost Kristen and Mike fell silent, lost in their own individual thoughts. The road ahead was filled with possibilities. Rows of sugarcane waved on the horizon. A small Jon boat with an outboard motor putted languidly in the sawgrass-lined canal beside the road. A buzzard flew lazy circles high above the road in search of fresh roadkill. They had travelled just far enough to be back in the land of cell phone coverage when Kristen's new phone chirped an incoming text. The message from Randoph, Grayson, and Gleason was a fraud alert. Someone had tried to access Dick Lance's old account. The warning ended by urging her to be on the alert for scammers. A new reality hit Kristen's brain like a breaking news bulletin.

"He's not dead," she blurted.

"Who's not dead?"

"Dick. My husband. He's not dead. I don't know how. He just tried to access his money. I know it. The bastard faked it."

"Don't jump to conclusions; think about where you are. This is Florida. Ground zero for fraud, hustlers, and dickweeds. Scumbags would try to sell you this swampland here as waterfront property ready for luxury homes. There are a million scammers and hackers out there."

Kristen pondered this.

"And besides," he said, staring intently. "Please, tell me truthfully, would it really matter to you now?"

'No, no I guess not. There's no going back."

Kristen gazed out over the endless acres of sawgrass and asked herself, knowing what she knew, what would Dick do? Then she remembered The Formula. It all came together in a flash like a carefully written direct response commercial script. The Problem...getting out of a failing marriage. The Secret...inky black swamp water that makes you vanish like

Magic! The Solution…call NOW to recoup your fortune and start a new life. Kristen turned to Mike and blurted out, "It's a dumb fox that don't have two holes to his burrow."

"Wait, what?"

"It's a saying from my father. Always have an out. He went in the water, but the asshole was just like his damn products; he was dishwasher safe!"

# CHAPTER 41

Mr. Hang Foo hung his suitcoat over his office chair and poured his afternoon cup of hot tea, a lifelong tradition he inherited from his parents. He stood gazing out his office window at downtown Newark and the Passaic River. He and his father had spent many an afternoon on the docks, hoping for a big catch with the Pocket Fisherman. He smiled at the memory. Now Hang Foo was hoping for an even bigger score with the Mega Meal A Gizer. He walked over to the glass display case where the miracle kitchen gadget basked in the glow of a tiny spotlight. He was finally acquitted of any wrongdoing, and his long-delayed two-minute TV commercial was up and running. As expected, it was an instant hit. He resolved to never do business with the treacherous Hong Kong syndicate again. The numbers were tremendous, but the money handlers were sucking up the lion's share of the profits.

Hang sat back down at his desk and turned his attention to his laptop. He brought up a rough cut of a commercial he was working on for a copper bracelet that was supposed to make aches and pains vanish. "Crippling arthritis pain keeping you down? Not anymore! Introducing Kopper Kryptonite!" He ran through the footage, making notes on what was working and what looked totally unbelievable. This kind of product had popped up in various forms many times over the years, so he needed to give it a fresh angle. He couldn't count on a big score with this one, but it could be a bread-and-butter product that would do reasonably well. He reviewed some footage of two wrinkled old men in tennis attire playing pickle ball. One geezer reached to make a shot and then doubled over in exaggerated pain. The expression on the actor's face looked ridiculous. The next take was even more comical. Hang sighed and made notes on a pad. He moved on to The Solution shots of the old guy wearing the bracelet and beaming with relief.

"Much better," he thought and started coming up with ad copy, mouthing the words as he wrote. "Has pickle ball become a pain? Pain in the pickle? Pickle pain makes you insane? Get powerful pickle pain relief!" He sat back in frustration and stared at his notes. Putting down his pen, he closed his eyes to meditate. Within a few seconds the telephone rang.

"Sir, you have a call from a Kristen Daniels," his secretary announced over the tinny speakerphone.

"I don't know a Kristen Daniels," he said. "Oh wait, that Kristen. I'll take that call."

"Mr. Hang Foo, I thought you'd remember me after all we've been through," chided Kristen.

Hang Foo smiled, "Of course, of course. Your maiden name threw me off. Kristen, I do hope you are well."

"I am, thank you. Better than well. And I know you're doing well because I can't get away from seeing that damn Mega Meal A Gizer nonstop on the cable stations. It's everywhere. But I'm in a new home now back in Columbus, Ohio, near my father."

"Ah, respect for your elders, I like that."

"And, surprise, surprise, I'm engaged."

"How wonderful! Such good news. Congratulations."

"I've opened an art gallery here, which I've always wanted to do. It's exciting, and it's going well. I'm back doing some op-ed pieces for the Dispatch every now and then, keeping my writing chops in, but the reason I'm calling is I wanted you to know that I'm starting another additional business, and I thought of you as a potential partner."

Hang Foo wasn't sure he had heard correctly. He paused a moment. "Partner? What kind of business are we talking about?"

"Direct Response, of course. Are you ready for another million seller? I'm already writing the script."

"To be honest, I'm on the verge of retiring. Getting out of the grind. I think you know why. This business can chew you up and spit you out. But, hey, absolutely, I'm always ready for new opportunities."

"I'm glad you don't hold my previous poor choice in men against me."

Hang Foo broke into a warm smile. "There is no reason that you and I can't help one another. Life is too short to be at odds. I am a reasonable man. As the philosopher says, we have two lives, and the second begins when you realize you only have one. So, what kind of product are you thinking of, Kristen? Thankfully, the old philosopher also says, "There's a sucker born every minute."

Kristen chuckled. "I'm pretty sure that was P.T. Barnum. Let me tell you about the amazing no-mess, no-fuss toy, guaranteed to make the kids scream with joy, the incredible Splatter Magic!"

# THE END

# ACKNOWLEDGMENTS

My sincere thanks to Mr. Tony Sammons, my high school speech teacher, who after having us do a simulated newscast, said, "You ought to think about doing this for a living". To all the recording studios in South Florida who helped get my kids through college and provided me with a free lunch until the internet came along and ruined in-person recording.

And to my lovely wife, who constantly showed her support whenever she saw me writing at my computer by saying, "Get off Facebook and do some chores".

# ABOUT THE AUTHOR

Rick Sheffield has been working in radio and television for over five decades and has voiced or created tens of thousands of commercials, some of them completely legitimate. Many of the outrageous events in this novel are based on personal experience; he just won't tell us which ones. If you are a regular TV watcher, there is a good chance you've heard his voice on an irritating commercial within the past week. Rick resides in South Florida with his wife, Leslie, and avoids the swamp whenever he can.

Made in United States
North Haven, CT
26 July 2024

55475245R00095